Things You Leave Behind

ML Kennedy

D1516933

ISBN: 978-1098884918

Cover Art by Andrew Sellers

DEDICATION

For Jen,

She knows what she did.

SOMEWHERE NEAR THE MIDDLE

Cliff had shaggy, lumpy hair, a shaggy, lumpy beard, and a shaggy, lumpy body. Though he looked unkempt, he always took pride in his punctuality. Cliff pulled out his phone and checked the time: 7:46. Maybe he was too early. He adjusted the volume of his audiobook and put the phone back into the pocket of his cargo shorts.

At 7:49, Cliff walked into "Grounds for Appeal" and ordered a medium black coffee in a to-go cup. He stared at a slice of pound cake but resisted temptation. The kid was already waiting for him, sitting in a corner table, sipping a chai latte in a for-here cup, and playing on a tablet. He was maybe eighteen years old, tall and lithe with olive skin. Cliff had recognized him from their previous encounter, but things were different now. The kid's hair was carefully styled and full of product, he was clean shaven, and he wore nicer clothes. It was so strange; just these minor differences in the way he presented himself made him seem like a completely different person.

A little voice inside Cliff's brain said, *"Well, that's the trick, isn't it?"*

The kid flagged him over, so Cliff smiled and complied, loudly declaring along the way, "Coffee's pretty good here, but these prices are higher than giraffe pussy. You know what I'm saying?"

The kid did not appear to know what the shaggy man was saying.

"So, Tyler," Cliff continued, taking a seat in the chair on the near side of the table. It wobbled, and Cliff replaced it with one from an adjacent table. "Sorry about that; you never want to be the fat guy that breaks a chair. Anywho, you remember me?"

Tyler froze for two blinks before realizing it was his turn to speak. "I remember. Well, I don't remember everything. It's like this twilight drugged state thing I was just reading about. Like when they keep people awake for surgery. It's like, you know," the kid paused, searching, "like remembering a dream." He looked away from Cliff, instead focusing on the thin layer of foam in his chai latte as it swirled around in his mug.

"Uh-huh." Cliff pulled at a few hairs growing out of his neck. "So, why'd you call me?"

Tyler took a deep breath, still not looking up from his drink. "Well, you know." He paused and took another breath. "I want to know about her."

"Her?" Cliff took the plastic lid off his coffee and watched the steam rise from the cup. He blew the steam and let it fog up his glasses.

"Her."

"Angela, right? You're talking about Angela. No need to be all mysterious, Tyler," Cliff said. "It's feels weird to call you Tyler. Sounds like a last name to me."

"Yeah," the kid replied, not knowing what to make of this strange man. Tyler watched as Cliff wiped his glasses dry with his faded green t-shirt.

"Uh-huh. You mind if I ask why?"

"What do you mean?" Tyler asked.

"Why do you want to know more about Angela?"

"What?" The answer seemed so obvious to Tyler. "Wouldn't you be curious? This whole situation has been so, um, screwed up."

"I'd say more fucked up than a football bat." Cliff enjoyed a drink of his coffee. It was not quite hot enough to burn his mouth if he took small sips. "Curiosity is natural, but how do you benefit from any of this? Why not just go on with your life? Weird shit happens, you move on."

"I am," came the reply, perhaps a bit too defensive. He restarted, "I will. But I want to record as much as possible, you know? I'm trying to," Tyler took a moment to find the phrasing he found least objectionable, "separate the memories from the dreams."

Cliff smiled. "Hell, you know I once woke up in between those two."

"Um, how do you mean?"

"A memory and a dream? I'm just quoting Tom Petty. It was a joke, son. Go on."

"Who is Tom Petty?"

"Christ Almighty, you are young." Cliff drank another sip of coffee waiting for the kid to continue. He didn't. He just sat there, squirming like a speeder waiting for the cop to approach his window. Cliff stared at the kid, then started, "I understand you've got questions. You should have some questions. I'm not sure that I'm the best choice to answer them, though. And it's not really my place to tell."

"Well, I just want to get as much of this story straight as I can, you know? It seemed least," another search for phrasing, "*awkward* to start with you, Cliff. I mean, your number was already in my phone. So, you answer my questions. I'll answer yours." The kid stared at the shaggy man and waited.

After what felt like a very long time, he got his answer. "No." Cliff carefully took a longer sip of his coffee. It had a nutty smell, with what might be hints of chocolate.

This did not compute. "What do you mean *no*?"

"I mean precisely that." The answer seemed so obvious to Cliff.

"I don't know where else to turn."

"These are private matters," Cliff declared. "I'm not going to air nobody else's dirty laundry."

The kid felt flush. He could feel his skin tightening. All he could think to say was, "That's not fair!"

"To who?" Cliff thought that maybe he would buy that pound cake. If he only ate half, he could eat the rest for breakfast.

11

"Cliff, please," Tyler paused, trying to reason. "Just at least think about it, okay? Just, well, why don't you give me your email address, and I'll ask some questions. I'm already familiar with these 'private matters.' I just need some semblance of clarity."

Cliff pulled a pen out of his coat pocket and pulled the sleeve off of his coffee. He wrote something down.

"You can ask me anything you want. I probably ain't gonna answer. I'd be willing to guess that just asking the questions will," Cliff grasped for the word on the tip of his tongue, but couldn't reach it. "It will make you feel a little better. That's all I can say."

Cliff left the sleeve on the table and the kid snatched it almost immediately. He pushed his tablet in a few spots before yelling towards the door. "Is this a G or a 6?"

Cliff had already exited the coffee shop. The word came to him a block later: Therapeutic.

He regretted not buying the pound cake.

Angela looked up at the clouds in the dark sky and just for a moment felt small and sad and alone. As a kid, just the thought of outer space filled her 2nd grade body with existential dread. The memories of those feelings felt so close right now, but passed quickly when Robert somehow splashed cold ocean water directly into her gym shoe. Annoyance replaced insignificance, and she made faces at Robert that went unnoticed in the dark.

She was pretty sure Robert was still talking to her, but her mind was on anything else. Robert had stopped moving for a moment to pull up his pants, so Angela balanced their cargo with her left hand and rubbed the back of her head with her right. She had just had her stylist chop off a bunch of

hair and loved how it felt in
the back. Getting a haircut
made her feel like a new
person, or at least it gave
this same old person a fresh
new start. She could use one of
those. She readjusted her grip
and stretched her back, looking
up at the moon. It seemed large
in the sky tonight even though
it was only a third full. *Do
they call it a third moon? Is
that a thing? Gibbous is a
moon word, right? I think that
means the opposite though.* She
remembered the difference
between waxing and waning, but
couldn't tell you which the
moon was up to presently.

They began walking once
again. Angela lost her balance
slipping on a wet stone,
thinking about the moon. She
nearly dropped her end of the
canoe.

*Gibbous, is that a hard or a
soft g?* She had only read the
word. She'd have to check the
dictionary when she got home.

Maybe she could also look up if they called them third moons.

The cool night air made goosebumps up and down Angela's arms and raised the freshly shorn hairs on the back of her neck. Angela wanted a warm bath, a cigarette, and winning lottery ticket; what she had was a chill from a damp wind, a canoe and Robert.

Robert. Robert was tall, slender and pretty enough that he seemed genuinely charming. Robert hadn't stopped talking since he loosened the straps of the car top carrier. He kept talking as he and Angela carried his uncle's canoe to the ocean; Angela knew that he had somehow stuck her with the heavier end, but he never stopped talking long enough for her to complain. Robert kept talking as he put on his life jacket and adjusted the straps of the vest to his long, ferret-like body. He kept talking when he took an off-balanced step into the canoe and nearly dumped Angela into the water.

Angela knew he was talking still when she used her paddle to push the canoe into deeper waters, but she could only catch about half of what he was saying over the noise of the waves. She had asked "what?" a few times, but decided that she didn't care enough to pursue that line of inquiry.

"I'm just saying that horror movies don't know what to do now that so many people are always carrying a cell-a-phone. They don't want to adjust to technology. They don't want to talk about the changes that information and communication technology bring. It's easier for them just to pretend that they don't exist. Do things the way they always have. They feel like it kinda wrecks the feeling of isolation by always being digitally connected. They don't realize that this is just a new form of isolation. So now we just get a bunch of situations where cell-a-phones never work in horror movies." It took quite a while for Robert to realize that he was now shouting his words in order to try to be louder than the ocean. He must have been shouting for some time as he felt the same tingle in his throat that he gets after a long night in a noisy bar.

Robert's spastic paddling brought a small yet noticeable amount of the sea into their canoe. Angela swept her wet bangs back and to the right. "I hadn't noticed that. So, have I ever told you that you get hella-gabby when you're nervous?" Angela yelled as she attempted to position their canoe away from a particularly jagged rock.

Robert didn't hear Angela's question, but it didn't deter him from answering. "Oh yeah. It's always NO SIGNAL is those big letters that no cell-a-phone I've ever used has ever had." Angela skillfully avoided

18

the rocks, but the bottom of the canoe scraped on a submerged branch. Robert seemed oblivious to the struggles of Angela and canoe alike. He rested his paddle across his lap, reached into his backpack to retrieve a flashlight and examined the sea-crag.

"You have good cell service?" Angela asked, shouting.

"Oh, I don't have a phone." Robert answered, shouting.

"Jesus fucking Christ. Then why are you complaining?" Angela questioned, shouting. By then the sea had quieted some.

"If I'm with a bunch of people, nowadays, at least half of them are going to have phones."

"So?"

"It lacks verisimilitude." Robert had only read that word before and hoped that he had pronounced it correctly.

"You don't know though. You'd be surprised how bad cell service is. I have to walk around my apartment just to get a signal. I went to Montana last year and had nothing in the whole state." She paused, thinking about those hours stuck in the car with Shannon. "Also, their coffee was shit." Angela was still angry about Montana's weak coffee some fourteen months later. She was expecting a thick sort of cowboy coffee, but instead was treated to warm murky water.

Robert took a deep breath to relax; Angela hadn't corrected his pronunciation of verisimilitude. Then he began again. "I mean, I understand that you can't get a signal everywhere, but I just saw it in, like, three movies in a row: *Identity*, *Wrong Turn* and something else. I just rented a bunch of movies. Blockbuster had a 'rent three for the price of two' deal. I ended up getting six. They all kinda sucked, though. *Freddy vs. Jason* was stupid, but kinda fun, I guess. *High Tension* was really good for a little while, but then had a dumb twist that didn't make any sense but was also obvious, if that's a thing? *House of 1000 Corpses* was, well, I'm not really sure what the hell that was."

"I still have a VCR." Angela knew that if Robert started talking about movies, he would never stop. She had hoped that saying she didn't even own a DVD player would provide the sort of social cue that Robert could follow.

"The Hollywood Video has a great VHS collection. They've got all sorts of great B movies like *Sorority Babes in the Slimeball Bowl-o-Rama* and *Coffy* and that George Romero movie where the guy who thinks he's a vampire calls up a radio show."

So, Angela was wrong. It was time for a new tactic. "Doesn't the bad guy in *Scream* use a cell phone?"

"Exception that proves the rule."

"That isn't what that expression means, Robert. It's talking about like when you see a sign that says 'No Parking 5a.m. to 7 a.m.' Because there is an exception, that means the rule is that you can park there the rest of the time."

"Whatever." Robert stared at the crag some more, studying where it met the water. "Where the hell did Cliff say we were supposed to park the canoe?"

"He didn't mention *parking* the canoe. Just find a spot where you can climb out," she commanded. "I'll toss you the rope and then I'll climb out. After that we'll just pull the canoe out of the water."

They did that thing, finding a spot illuminated by the

glowing sign of a Pizza Castle restaurant on the shore.

"Do you think I should I take the oar with me?" Robert released the three buckles from its belts, shimmied out of the life vest, and tossed it into the canoe.

"You don't have an oar," Angela corrected. "It's a paddle." Robert scowled at her; she pretended not to notice. "Why would you want the paddle?" Angela had seen Robert pack his bag with a drill, three different types of screwdriver, a chisel, two hammers, a pry bar, a giant bag of trail mix, three water bottles, and a fire blanket. Angela, on the other hand, hadn't even remembered to bring a life jacket.

"We're going to an abandoned lighthouse in the middle of the night. This is creepy central. Weren't half the episodes of 'Scooby Doo' about creepy lighthouses?" As if on cue, a cool wind blew on Robert. He put up the hood of his sweatshirt and pulled down on its lace until only his nose poked out.

Angela furrowed her brow. "I mostly remember carnivals." She looked at her left wrist. "Also, it's like 10:15." She wasn't actually wearing a watch; she had forgotten that as well. But she was pretty sure it was no later than quarter after ten.

"Stop being so argumentative," Robert snapped.

"Stop being so wrong and/or full of bullshit."

"Are you sure we never dated?" Robert asked.

"Since I'm not a gay boy," Angela said, "I'm pretty sure the answer is no."

"I'm bi-sexual, Angela."

"Really?" Angela contorted her face in a peculiar way.

"Yeah. You didn't know that?" Robert declared, "I've made out with, like, two girls in high school."

"Oh, but you don't find me attractive?"

"I, uh-"

Angela smiled and attempted to throw her arm around Robert and mess up his hair in a big sisterly manner, but his hood was up and he was too damned tall. "You're too damned tall, anyway," she said.

"I wasn't trying to be," replied Robert in his best Humphrey Bogart voice.

"You're shaking. Are you cold?"

"No."

"You're really scared of a lighthouse?" Angela asked.

"Kinda. Well, you heard what Cliff told me."

"Which thing? Cliff talks a lot." Robert talked too much when he was nervous. Cliff talked too much when awake. Why did everybody in her life talk so damned much?

"You know," Robert responded trying to force the words out, "about how after they closed this place as a lighthouse, they used it as a columbarium?"

"Yeah, but I don't know what that word means." She fished a cigarette from her jacket pocket and a lighter from her bra. Angela remembered to bring the important things.

"It's where people go to dump ashes."

"Ashes?" She lit the cigarette.

"Spooky dead people ashes. Like, cremated remains." Robert held the paddle in his right hand and stared at it.

"Spooky dead people?"

"Well the spooky ashes of dead people." Robert moved the paddle to his left hand and stared at it.

"It's called a columbarium?"

"Yeah." Robert set the paddle in the canoe, picked it back up, and then hesitated with it in his hand. He bit his lip and pondered.

"But they cremate 'em and they don't bury 'em?" Angela stared at Robert staring at the canoe. "Just leave the fucking paddle, Robert. C'mon let's get on with this."

"Fine. But only because I don't think a paddle would hurt a ghost." Robert grabbed the flashlight back out from his bag, banged the bottom and twisted it on.

"Yeah, but an oar might."

"Ha ha." He shined his flashlight up and down the tower.

"So, burnt dead people got you creeped out?"

"A little bit."

"Maybe we could turn on that big nightlight up there," Angela joked as they headed toward the lighthouse.

"Naw, they removed the lens like ten years ago. I tell you what, I'd bet that there is no cell signal here."

"Dunno. I left my phone in the car." Angela flicked ashes off her cigarette. She took a drag and now enjoyed the night sky, the cool ocean air, and the silence. Then she had to ruin it. "But the question remains: Do you think Nine-one-one would send out first responders against the Blob?"

Robert laughed. "Why the Blob?" Robert stared at the lighthouse, waiting for an electrical storm or, at the very least, some rain. He was sure that in the movies a

thunderstorm would show up
right around now. "This is,
like, ghost pirate territory or
Lovecraftian terror stuff."

"It's just the scariest
movie I've ever seen."

"Really?"

"Totally." Angela took a
long drag off her cigarette,
and held the smoke in her
lungs.

Waves crashed over the side
of the crag as Robert and
Angela walked around to the
front of the lighthouse. The
door was boarded shut.

"Which version of *The Blob*
did you see?" Robert kneeled in
front of it and took off his
backpack.

"What?" Angela snapped on
her lighter to illuminate the
bag, and Robert soon found his
electric drill.

"Did you see the old one
with Steve McQueen or the one

from, like, fifteen years ago with Kevin Dillon?" He twisted the end of the drill.

"I saw the one from the 80s with the guy from the old 'Law and Order's. But I think I saw part of one from the 70s, too, where either Laverne or Shirley plays a hippie that gets blobbed." Angela touched the locket around her neck. It felt cold in her fingers.

"That's- Never mind." As he pushed the Phillips head bit into the drill, Robert asked, "Did you know some people have a 'girls turning into slime' fetish?"

"What?"

"There are people who are turned on by the blob, I guess."

"Why would that even be a thing?" Angela was incredulous.

"Some dudes like their balls stepped on by high heels. I don't understand anybody." The drill screamed as he removed screw after screw.

"You and me both, sister," she said to him.

"I just like the porn where pretty people wear not much clothing."

"Mostly boys?"

"Mostly men," he corrected.

The last screw fell to the ground, but the board remained. Robert examined the situation. "I think the humidity warped the wood." He pushed in a few spots to see if it would give.

"Let me try."

"Hold on."

"Just let me try," Angela commanded.

"Okay fine. Sheesh," Robert conceded.

Angela put her cigarette between her lips, and kicked the board with the bottom of

her foot. It creaked forward.
She did it again. The board
cracked slightly and creeped
forward a little more.

The third kick did it in.

Angela's locket had swung
around to her back during her
brief martial art exposition.
She fixed it and then attempted
a smoke ring, unsuccessfully.
She motioned *after you* to
Robert.

Robert fixed the flashlight
into his right hand and held it
next to his face. He carefully
illuminated every possible area
he could, searching for ghost
pirates or Lovecraftian beasts
before finally squeezing his
way into the lighthouse.

He examined the lighthouse
from the inside now, shining
the flashlight across walls and
floor, stone by stone. He
discovered bugs of various
shapes and sizes, watching them
skitter away from his light.

"We're going to die here, aren't we?" Robert asked this, unsure whether or not he was kidding.

Angela stubbed out her cigarette on a wet rock. "Meh," she responded.

"You know, right before this place opened in 1879, there was, like, this big shipwreck here. Like, a dozen people died."

"I guess they needed a lighthouse," concluded Angela. It didn't seem too dark tonight though. *Probably from light pollution from the city*, Angela thought remembering that term from "The Simpsons."

"It's more than that, Angie. This place is seriously haunted. Something like six of the lighthouse keepers died going out here. Eventually they decided to close the place, because the people kept dying."

"Who is they? What a bunch of nonsense."

"Well, I don't know. Whoever it was were the same guys who sold it to the columbarium people. And then that-"

"Over here." Angela's face was glowing from her lighter as she flagged over Robert. "Read this stone."

"1911. So what? It's the foundation stone."

"You just said this place was built in 1879."

"Shit. Maybe it's a code. 1911. . . Uh, Colt 1911. Maybe look to see if there are bricks shaped like a gun?"

"Or," Angela said as she grabbed the pry bar from Robert's bag. She gouged it into the mortar, "we take a closer look at the brick." She scraped and wedged and torqued and twisted. She stopped abruptly and turned to Robert.

"Foundation stone isn't like a keystone, right?"

"Sort of." He hesitated a moment and then realized what Angela meant. "Oh, but you're not going to bring the lighthouse down on our head, if that is what you're thinking."

"That's good to know," she replied, resuming her scraping and wedging and torqueing and twisting.

"You want a hand?"

"Fuck off, patriarchy!" She paused. Robert raised an eyebrow at Angela; she smirked back at him. "No thanks, I feel it starting to move." Angela wedged the bar in the side of the stone, and pushed.

Suddenly there was a hole in the side of the lighthouse.

"What's in there?" Robert asked. "Is it the ring? Do you think it could actually be the ring?"

"Jesus fucking Christ, just let me look."

Angela stuck her arm into the hole.

Something was in there. Maybe it was the ring. She couldn't tell; everything felt wet and mossy.

"Can you get it?"

"I'm trying. Back off." Angela could feel something barely within her reach. She stretched far enough to touch it with the tips of her fingers, cutting her knuckle on a rock in the process. "Hand me a screwdriver," she commanded Robert.

He complied.

With the screwdriver, she was able to slide whatever it was just a little bit closer. She reset and pulled it within her grasp.

"I think I've got it," she told Robert.

Angela was running late.

She hated running late.

Running late was the worst.

Angela was running late because the girl who was supposed to be taking over her shift at the register was running late. Running late didn't seem to bother Kim. Every day, Kim was seven to thirteen minutes late. It sounds petty and crazy to not round those numbers off to the nearest five, but this job was making Angela petty and crazy.

This was the survival job that Angela worked to have extra money in college. Then, after she graduated, it was the survival job to pay the bills until she got that job where she would use her college degree.

38

But here she was, still going on interviews a year after graduation, still working this same crummy job at the same crummy mall. If Kim showed up soon, Angela would still have time. She could get changed at the food court bathroom, freshen up a bit, and maybe grab a burrito to eat in the car. She had planned on taking time to sit down, eat lunch and prepare for the interview, but she no longer had that time to spare.

She no longer had seven of those minutes.

Eight of those minutes.

Nine of those minutes.

Te-no still nine of those minutes.

Okay, now ten of those minutes. Ten goddamned minutes.

Ten Goddamned Minutes.

I'm fucking leaving this bitch if she doesn't show up soon.

Fuck this place.

Kim showed up to work twelve minutes late with her clothes disheveled and her hair looking like a bird's nest after a thunderstorm. "You would not believe the morning I've had! My boyfriend calls me and wakes me up at nine in the morning, when I had just gone to bed at three. And he's all-"

Kim lugged a giant, yellow purse and three bags of who-knows-what onto the counter and then started shoving each of them in whatever space she could find underneath the register.

"And you would not believe what he has the nerve to say to me!"

"Sure wouldn't, Kim. Gotta go." Angela tossed the bag of her interview clothes over her

40

shoulder and hopped out of the store. She made a beeline for the restrooms.

The first stall was gross, but the second stall was for the handicapped. So, Angela flushed the toilet with her foot and did her best to keep her interview clothes off of the floor. She had soaked the toes of her knee-highs in a puddle that she was ninety percent sure was water.

Or at least the puddle was ninety percent water.

She stared at the mirror, ran a brush through her dark brown hair, adjusted her locket on its chain, and checked her mascara and lipstick. She was hoping that mascara and lipstick were enough makeup to pass as a professional working adult. She didn't really care for any of that other stuff.

Pleased enough by her appearance, Angela went to the food court and quickly assessed which line would move the fastest. She was out of luck when it came to her burrito; in fact, her top two places to go were packed. She was stuck with the mediocre burger chain. Her favorite menu items here were too messy to eat in the car, so she opted for a simple cheeseburger.

She plotted her revenge on Kim.

Angela quickly went to the parking lot to find her 1988 Ford Tempo, affectionately named Gomez. Gomez was always easy to find as his quarter panels were a different color from his bumper which was yet a different color from his doors. She slid into the driver seat, and looked over the two pages of MapQuest directions printed out entirely in red because her printer was out of black ink. Satisfied that she knew *about* where to go, she went about starting the car and eating her third-choice burger from her third-choice restaurant. They had forgotten her pickles, again.

Somehow, she knew that her lack of pickles was also Kim's fault. Her mind raced trying to figure out how she had done it.

A blue Dodge blew through a stop sign as Angela pulled out of the mall parking lot. She swerved and smashed down on her horn. For a moment, she was proud that she didn't end up with a blouse full of hamburger. But then she was distracted by a noise.

Was it a fire truck?

Was it some sort of alarm?

Aw crap.

Apparently, "horn" could be added to the list of the things dying in Gomez the '88 Tempo. Well, that wasn't quite fair. The horn definitely worked. In fact, it wouldn't stop working. Angela drove down the road and punched at Gomez's steering wheel until the noises ceased.

It only took about a third of a
mile and about fourteen
punches.

Angela finished her burger
and threw the wrapper into the
paper bag on the seat. It was
then that she noticed the
mustard. Somehow and somewhere
in her frenzy, she had dribbled
a long stream of mustard down
the front of her interview
blouse.

And so, Angela drove the
next eight miles attempting to
suck the stain out of her
blouse while steering. She
thought she had done a good
enough job of sucking the
yellow out, but now the blouse
had a weird wet spot.

Angela pulled into the
parking garage of the office
building. A portly man with a
van dyke handed her a ticket
and raised the barrier gate to
let her in. He was better
dressed than she was. For a
moment he looked like Chris
Kozminsky. Angela once went to

a high school dance with Chris Kozminsky. His dad was a toll booth operator. Maybe that's a career opportunity she overlooked.

Angela wondered if she had the four dollars to pay the lot fee. Maybe they'd validate. She spun the car around in circles, carefully reading for whom all the empty spots were reserved. Maybe all the spots would be full, and she could just go home watch TV and take a long bath.

She found an empty spot in P3 and stared at the ugly concrete walls. Jesus, it looked like a dungeon in there. She took three deep breaths and went to find room 701-D, trying her best to look like a real and responsible adult. Angela talked to building security, and sure enough 701-D was on the seventh floor. She gave the guard a half smile and said "lucky seven" as he pointed her toward the elevator.

Something made a weird noise as she walked. She was alone in the elevator and had a chance to check it out. The sole of her discount retailer brand shoes had come unglued from the imitation leather. Her flats were nearly flip-flops. Oh well, at least she was five minutes early. That much of her day had gone right. She fidgeted nervously with her locket and took another deep breath outside of 701-D. Angela checked in with a receptionist and stole a piece of tape from the dispenser on his desk.

Angela sat in an ugly maroon chair and rolled the tape around her finger, sticky side out. She crossed her legs and surreptitiously snuck the tape between shoe and heel.

Well, that's slightly less terrible.

The receptionist called Angela's name which somehow caused all of Angela's blood to attempt to leave her body through her feet.

The man who interviewed Angela was really nice, or maybe he was an octopus. She couldn't remember anything about him. She did remember that he asked all those annoying interview questions like, "Why did you apply for this position?" and "Where do you see yourself in five years?" She knew "money" and "I wish I knew" were the wrong responses to give, but couldn't guarantee that what she ended up telling him was any better.

Angela also remembered hearing a sound like an ambulance or a fire alarm when he asked her about her greatest weaknesses and strengths. The noise continued as he asked her about how she has displayed her leadership in the past.

She realized that the noise was coming from Gomez right before he asked her, "Do you have any questions for me?"

"Um, do you validate?"

After the interview, Angela
hurried back to Gomez. The horn
was still going off, but
sounding sickly. She punched it
over and over again. Nothing
happened for the longest time.
Finally, thirty punches later,
the horn made a comical dying
sound and the parking garage
became delightfully quiet. She
found two dollars in her wallet
and had enough change in the
plastic dip in front of the
shifter to make the other two.
What was that space meant for,
anyway? Was it for change?

Angela waited until she
stepped through her front door
before she unhooked her bra.
She threw it on the floor as
she kicked the door closed.
Angela flung herself onto the
couch and turned the television
on to a syndicated judge show.
She stared at the television
while absent-mindedly ripping

the heels off her interview
shoes.

Twenty minutes later she
turned her attention to the big
black cordless phone which she
had purchased last month from
the drug store. The red LED
informed her that she had three
messages; the first two ended
up being from her sister.

Message one began. "Hey,
it's just me. It's quiet over
here, and I thought I'd check
in on you. How's the job hunt
going? I can put out a few
leads for you if you'd like. I
know people. Gosh, it seems
like we've been playing phone
tag for a long time now. Well,
you know the drill, little sis,
I'm here if you need me."

A sizable pause.

"So. Uh, yeah."

BEEP.

Message two started *in
medias res*. "It's hard for me.
I'm out here and I feel all

alone. I feel like I don't have anybody to go to when things go wrong, you know? I'm working without a net. I just want you to know that you don't have to. I'm your net. I'm a net, like Annette Benning. Heh. You don't have to put up with these, these things I put up with. Heh. I'm sorry, I'm a little buzzed right now. I'm buzzing because I don't have a net to keep the buzzing out. Ha!

"But you know, you got me, and I got you, but I'm the big sister. You're the not big sister. I'm taller than you, still. Remember that too."

BEEP.

"Jesus Christ, Shannon, it's the middle of the afternoon."

The not-Shannon message was from Robert. "Hey. It's only me. Nothing important."

Angela started dialing the phone.

"Jell-o," came the voice on the other end.

"Hey. It's Angela."

"Yeah."

"I can't believe it's come to this."

"Uh-huh. What's up?" Cliff asked, sounding distracted.

"I'm in. I'll go to your stupid fucking lighthouse and look for your stupid fucking diamond." Angela could hear Cliff shift in his chair. She knew it was the sound of him starting to pay attention to this conversation.

"All right. I knew you'd come to your senses. What about Robert?"

"I'll deal with him," she said, resigned to this fate.

"Three-way split on the money sound fair?"

"Jesus fucking Christ. Cliff, do you actually think we'll find something?"

"As the mastermind of this operation, I must prepare for every contingency, Angela." She could hear his smile over the phone.

"Ugh, fine. Three-way is fine."

"You been angling for a three-way, you damned sex pervert."

"Shut up Cliff," Angela responded automatically.

"Heh, you know what I just realized?"

"What now?"

"I'm the Charlie Xavier of this mission. You're Angela. You're Charlie's Angela." Cliff attempted to sing the notes to the "Charlie's Angels" pre-commercial music cue, but was typically tone deaf.

"Cliff, my day has been hella-shitty. Do you want me to do this or not?"

"Yes ma'am. I'm sorry."

"All right."

"It's just, how long we known each other? How has Charlie's Angela never come up before?"

"Because your name isn't really Charlie. It's only Charlie in this fantasy within a fantasy in your head."

"Well, still. What else have we been missing all these years?"

"I'm just going to hang up now, okay?" It wasn't an idle threat.

"I was gonna let you be Kate Jackson."

"You're damn right I'm Sabrina. That's not even a question." Angela maneuvered

the phone into its big, black
cradle.

ONE

"He was battling this for 20 years."

Angela was in and out.

"We've seen it a couple of times. We've seen it with Whoopi Goldberg and we've seen it with him."

She tried to open her eyes, but having them closed felt so good. Maybe just another twenty minutes of sleep.

"They are confirming that he did pass away. Of course, our hearts, our thoughts and our prayers go out-"

She was itchy. Everything felt itchy and numb at the same time. Her legs were itchy. Her face was itchy. Her left hand felt weird.

"-and we're all running back to our desks-"

Was there tape? Why would there be tape on her hand? Why was it so pokey?

"Quicken loans can pay your mortgage for an entire year!"

She must've been in a hospital. It smelled like a hospital. She felt nauseated. Whatever was on her felt like hospital sheets, that weird industrialized attempt at comfort.

"Now get 0 percent financing for 16 months-"

She tried to open her eyes. They burned. It took a while to focus. A few slow blinks helped, but everything was blurry. Angela reached for her locket but couldn't find it.

"Press a button and relaxing pulses-"

Okay it looks like a hospital, too. Everything was

still fuzzy, so she squinted.
Angela saw a smartly-dressed,
pear-shaped woman in a blue
blazer. She looked like one of
those hospital staffers that
never dealt with the messy
stuff, like a lawyer or a
dietician. The woman glanced in
Angela's direction, smiled an
open-mouthed smile, turned off
the television and hurried out
of the room. Angela decided
that the woman in the blazer
was a lawyer. That seemed
right. Like a white Mrs.
Huxtable.

Maybe five more minutes'
sleep. That would probably
help.

What's going on?

Angela looked at the
television. It was a flat
screen mounted on the top
corner of the room. This must
be a rich person hospital. You
think rich people could afford
a non-blurry TV. And non-blurry
chairs. And even her hands

looked blurry and weird. She closed her eyes again.

Angela opened her eyes again, wondering, *do I have insurance for this?* The last thing she could remember was reaching into the wall of the lighthouse. Everything was foggy. The ring! The ring was important, right? Did she have the ring? She remembered feeling something in the wall. Was it the ring? Was it a seahorse?

She needed a few more seconds to rest.

Why am I in the hospital? Did the lighthouse collapse when I pulled out the foundation stone? Stupid Robert, thinks he knows about lighthouses. Where is he anyway?

She must have slept a little more. When Angela opened her eyes again, she saw a blonde woman in green scrubs and a white lab coat standing next to her bed. "How are we doing?" the doctor asked.

Angela was surprised she could make a noise at all. Her throat felt like it was bleeding. "I don't know about us, but I feel like hammered shit," she said. Her voice was hoarse.

"Language!" the lawyer snapped at her. She was standing at the foot of the bed, studying Angela.

"Fuck you, lady, all right?" was Angela's response. She had tried to yell it, but it came out more like a whispered moan. "Can I have some water?" She desperately wanted a drink of water, but didn't think about trying to swallow it.

"The nurse is coming with some ice chips."

"I feel weird."

"Well, you collapsed out there. We're still trying to figure out exactly what

happened. You got a pretty
nasty bump on your head."

"I don't remember hitting my
head."

"Yeah, that pretty common
with head injuries. Tell me,"
the doctor asked, "do you
remember me telling you my
name?"

"No. I don't think you did."
Angela's mind was starting to
feel sharper, even if her
vision was still fuzzy.

"I'm Dr. Stephens," she
said, automatically pointing to
the badge clipped to the pocket
of her lab coat. "Do you know
your name?"

"Of course, I do. Okay,
you're Doctor Stephens. I can
remember that. I'll think about
'Bewitched' and Samantha."

"Can, you please tell me
your name?"

"Angela Brooks."

"Angela Brooks?" the lawyer repeated, sounding incredulous.

"Oh, you've heard of me?" Angela joked.

"Ms. Clark, could I ask you to step outside for a moment?" The lawyer, named Ms. Clark apparently, reluctantly obeyed Dr. Stephens. The doctor focused her attention back to Angela. "Mothers. . ."

That word stung Angela, but she tried not to let it show on her face. "She looks pretty young to be your mom."

"Can you tell me what day it is?"

"Well, I don't really know. It looks like I've been out a day or so. So, I'm guessing that it's tomorrow night."

"Which would make it. . ."

"Why was Ms. Clark here? Am I in trouble for trespassing? I assumed the lighthouse was public property, and I think my record is pretty clean." Angela wanted to ask if Robert was here. She wanted to ask about the ring. But if there are lawyers involved maybe there are cops around. Even loopy with a blow to the head, she knew enough not to tip her hand. *No point in getting Robert in trouble, or telling other people about the ring, especially if we found something out there.*

"Please answer my question, and then maybe I can help you out with some answers. Okay?"

"Am I under arrest?"

"No."

"Then, I say it is Thursday, September 9, 2004. What do I win?"

The doctor wrote a few things down on her pad. "Listen, I'm going to step outside for just a minute. Okay? I'll be right back, I promise. Okay?"

"Yeah, fine whatever." Angela was angry about the noticeable lack of answers from this doctor, but mostly she just wanted to go back to sleep. Maybe just a few more minutes. She felt weak. She felt thin. How long had she been in the bed? Why did the doctor react like that?

Everything felt . . . off.

Wasn't it Thursday?

She was so tired. Angela gathered enough strength to scratch around the tape on her left hand. So tired. Some sort of tube was growing out of there, out of her hand. Why was she so tired? She glanced up at the clear liquid bag suspended above her and to the left before falling back asleep.

In her dreams, she could hear the doctor and the lawyer talking. "We're going to do an MRI, just to make sure there is no bleeding on the brain and that everything is getting oxygen in there, okay?"

"What is all this stuff? What's with Angela?"

"We'll figure it out. Listen, I don't know if the MRI is going to find anything, okay? It might and we'll see what we do from there. In case it doesn't, I'm just going to schedule, um, Dr. Kassir in here from Neurology for a consult."

Angela dreamed that she and her sister, Shannon, were going to the high school from the TV show "Boy Meets World". Topanga was being a real bitch. Screech was there, but he wasn't supposed to be.

Why is Shannon in the same classes as me? Did she fail a couple of years or something? Why is Topanga so mean to Screech?

She woke up feeling cloudy, but stronger.

She poked around her head, trying to get a read on how big a goose egg was back there. *My hair still feels short; must not have been out for too long.* Something plastic tugged at her ear when she moved her hand back down.

It was a hospital bracelet. She had to squint to read it.

Patient: Clark, Tyler
Adm: 08/11/14

Dob: 09/13/96   Age: 17 years   M

Dr. STEPHENS MD, MELISSA K

St. Vincent Medical Center

Angela suddenly felt very awake.

"I may be an atheist and a liar, but this right here is the god's honest truth. It all started in 1905, when this lawyer named Edward Bloch started making a series of very wise investments. He worked night and day, tirelessly, for the next five years. People used to say he would sleep eight hours a week. He even got run over by a horse, and worked from the hospital bed."

"He got run over by a horse?"

"It's old time-y times; that sort of thing happened. He walked with a cane after that, but that just helped his old time-y rich person image. He probably even had those old time-y foot cover things like Scrooge McDuck."

"Spats."

"Sure. Whatever. So, 1910 rolls along and Edward Bloch is one of the richest men in the country, but he's bored. He takes a step back from his work, delegates his business and investments and all that shit to some underlings. This sumbitch is off to live off the fat of the land, the life of goddamned leisure. Well, it turns out that he hates golf, he hates sailing, and he really hates horses. The horse thing is totally understandable, what with being run over by one and all.

"So, in 1911 he does what any sane man would do, he tracks down the prettier, younger sister of his high school sweetheart and proposes to her."

"Jesus Christ!"

"Well, I don't know if they went to high school together and if they even called it high school in old time-y times, but you know, Edward Bloch and

Samantha Feller dated as teenagers and now he proposes to her sister Helen. As you may remember, girls named Helen are historically dangerous to powerful men.

"And in true crazy rich guy fashion, he commissions a ring to be made out of this five carat blue diamond valued at somewhere between fifty and a hundred and fifty thousand dollars. 1911 dollars, mind you. This stone was, I guess, sorta famous because it was one of the first ones measured after they standardized the carat in 1907. Before that, I guess it was the wild, wild west. On top of all this, everything I looked up called the diamond 'fancy' and that's gotta be good, right? It is bona fide fancy, like Heinz goddamn ketchup.

"So he proposes, and she says 'yes' and a lot of people say it was for the money or the ring and some people say it was because they had always loved

each other even when he was
dating the sister, which is
really gross because she was,
like, nine at that time. Me, I
say it was because she just
wanted to ditch the name Helen
Feller."

"Is old time-y times also
Helen Keller times?"

"Yeah, her autobiography
was, like, 1903. Did you know
she is credited with, uh,
starting the Akita breed in
America? That's true. Well, I
mean she didn't start it, or
have sex with a dog or grow it
in a lab or something, she was-
"

"Cliff, get on with it."

"Yeah, yeah. Anyways,
prohibition hits the Blochs
hard. Bloch's people had
invested a bunch into alcohol
manufacturers. Pretty much all
those companies died in 1920,
except for the ones big enough
to bleed money for thirteen
years or however long that shit

lasted. Edward Bloch doesn't know whether to crap or wind his watch. He is scrambling, and meanwhile Helen Bloch goes all William Randolph Hearst and starts buying everything in the catalogue. That's not an expression, but I feel it should be. She is blowing money like a hundred goddamned drunken sailors. Then bam, 1923, she gets diphtheria, her lymph nodes swell and close her throat. She's dead as a doornail. Eddie was trying to get some deal done in New York, and since it's still old time-y, it takes him a week to get back. It's all stress and bullshit and more stress."

"The standard bullshit sandwich on fresh stress?"

"You know it. So, Ed buries Helen. Then he turns around and files a report that her big blue ring is gone. He's fighting with the insurance company for, like, eighteen months. At the time, people were saying that he buried the ring with her and is trying to scam the insurance. He owes money to a bunch of people, and there is even some talk of gangsters. Gangsters were prevalent during prohibition. Those sumbitches were everywhere wearing hats and shooting damn tommy guns."

"Wearing pin-striped suits.
. ."

"Pinstriped Goddamned suits! Almighty! But I digress. Bloch dies before he can collect any insurance money. Some parade horse went nuts, broke her reins, ran like ten miles and trampled him while he was reading a newspaper in the park."

"Bullshit."

"Horses apparently hated this guy even more than he hated them. I shit you not. So, he's got no kids, his wife's dead, and the government seizes whatever else he had. The name Edward Bloch dies right after the man. All that's left of him is the mystery of the big blue ring. It is Bigfoot. It is Nessie."

"I thought you had pictures of bigfoot?"

"That ain't neither here nor there. In the 50s, some jerk-hole is convinced that it was buried with Helen and files a petition to exhume the body. The government says no. Jerk-hole shows up there with a shovel anyway, and the cops throw him in the clink before he even gets three feet under. He gets out, waits a year, tries again. Well, it's a deep dark night, and jerk-hole digs up the wrong damned body. As it turns out, the remains of the honorable judge John Bunyan Sellers didn't have any damned rings on it. But he did have some nephews on the police force who made sure that Jerk-hole couldn't even carry a shovel anymore.

"So, nobody knows where the ring is, and if they do, they aren't going to tell nobody about it. See, rumor goes around that one of the big crime families has called the mafia version of 'dibs' on this thing. Bloch screwed them out of hundreds of thousands of dollars by dying before paying. So, if anybody does show up with this ring, he's going to be sleeping with Luca Brasi.

"70s comes along, and some dipshit from Wisconsin is pretending to be a Hungarian Count, and he sells three fake big blue rings to even bigger dipshits in San Fran, San Diego and LA. Then, he tries that shit in Nevada. Well, the cops find what's left of him in a fountain on the strip."

"Bellagio?"

"Who am I, Wayne Newton? How the fuck should I know? This takes us all the way to 1985. An old man dies. He was a tailor. He went blind. He was a widower who was married to the same woman for fifty years. Nothing special, right? The nurse says his last words were 'I gave the ring to Nora.' His dead wife was named Eleanor, he's got dementia, no big deal, right?

"Except that in the fifty some odd years they were together, he only called his wife 'Ellie.' Everybody called her 'Ellie.' Why would he call her something else after she died? Dementia? That don't make any sense, but it's good enough for almost everybody. It does, however, bother the son, so he goes asking around. He digs up diaries, talks to a bunch of octogenarians, tries to find whatever he can find. Seems like a dead end. Who the hell is Nora? Did his father have a mistress? Did his father have some sort of twisted Eleanor fetish?

"Some kids care a lot if their parents cheated on each other. I don't really understand that. My mom fucked the drycleaner. My dad fucked a different drycleaner. I thought my house was normal. You're an adult, you get settled down, have a family, and fuck a drycleaner."

"Cliff, focus."

"Anywho, so the son's research tells him that his dad had one girlfriend before his mom. Some girl named Tilly who worked as a maid. He writes that off as a dead end, and collects the old peoples' stories on a website, that my mom linked me to because she thinks it's cute. This is what she does. She doesn't fuck drycleaners anymore; she reads the GeoCities pages of strangers. As the fella says, it's sure a drag it to get old."

"That's not how the song goes."

"So, I check out this asshole's site. Turns out Tilly

wasn't just any maid, she was, hold up, the Blochs' maid around 1922. Me and my brain here have a good old fashioned come-to-Jesus meeting, and I start thinking, what if "the ring" is *the* ring. What if Tilly ended up with the ring, somehow? I don't know, maybe she finds old Helen dead and pries it off her finger. Maybe she grabs it out of the sock drawer; I guess the how doesn't really matter.

"So, let's say Tilly has the big blue ring and realizes that if she tries to sell it, she'll end up dead or in jail or dead in jail. She has a panic attack, in old time-y times, back before they called them panic attacks. Tilly gives the ring to her old boyfriend, the tailor.

"But the tailor wasn't a tailor then. No, no. Before he was a tailor, he was a lighthouse keeper for the lighthouse at MacArthur bay. So he figures, 'shit nobody is going to find this ring out here.' So, he stashes the ring in the lighthouse. He's there for hours at a time by himself, so he can hide it where nobody can find it. He's got enough time in there to tunnel out of Shawshank. Not an expression, but I think it should be."

"What makes you think the ring is at the lighthouse?"

"Because MacArthur bay wasn't MacArthur bay before General MacArthur. Back then it was called Norville bay. And guess what they used to call the lighthouse?"

Robert felt the need to answer out loud. "Nora." Angela did not feel this need, instead rolling her eyes involuntarily.

"So here's the plan for the yearly Kurtwood Smith day adventure," Cliff declared. "We bust into the MacArthur Bay lighthouse, find a giant blue diamond, and *we* live off the fat of the goddamned land."

"Two things," Robert countered. "One, Kurtwood Smith day kinda already passed."

"Bullshit." Cliff interrupted. "Kurtwood Smith day is when we decide it is. Have we ever actually done it in July?"

"Kurtwood Smith day exists not in a calendar, but in our hearts, Robert," Angela explained.

"Well, and two, you just had knee surgery and don't appear to be up for any of this. Two point five, that lighthouse is creepy as shit."

"I know I can't physically lead the charge to battle. I'm planning and controlling this mission from a wheelchair, like Charles Xavier or Niles Caulder."

"Niles Caulder? That's a deep pull."

Angela pinched the bridge of her nose with her right hand

and chuckled. "Cliff," she began, "I've got work and job interviews and bills and adult shit to worry about. I don't have time to fuck around to be your surrogate adventurer."

"Hold up-"

"No, look, this is your Sasquatch thing and your ghost hunter thing all over again."

Robert interjected, "Well, I liked the Sasquatch thing, but this is sounding a lot like your ill-fated 'let's sleep in the cemetery' adventure."

"Oh my god, what a bunch of babies! I remember when Kurtwood Smith day used to mean something to you guys." Cliff continued, "Hold up. Just think about it for a day or two. You don't have to say yes, but just don't say no right now. Okay?"

Enough time elapsed for a deep breath for Angela and a deep breath for Robert.

"All right."

TWO

Angela was genuinely
surprised to wake up ten years
in the future in the body of a
teenage boy. As is the case
with many things, Denial was
the first stage. Surely her
head was cloudy from the
painkillers and this was all a
hallucination. Or maybe she
read the bracelet wrong in all
of that cloudiness. She
checked the bracelet again
before checking other things.

Well, maybe the bracelet was
wrong.

Nope, this was definitely a
teenage boy body.

Angela felt all around her
face, checking her head for
virtual reality equipment,
Matrix wires or something.
There was nothing like that,
but her face did feel wrong in

her hands and her hands felt wrong on her face.

She tried to go back to sleep. That would reset everything, right? Like unplugging an electronic device, slowly counting to ten and plugging it back in.

Unsurprisingly, Angela found it very difficult to get back to sleep. Instead, her body became overwhelmed with panic.

Angela sat up as best she could and shook her head, or maybe it was Tyler's head. She saw a telephone on the table next to her, but didn't know who to call. *Can I call 911? I'm already in a hospital! Shannon? Dad? If this is the future, I hope they still have the same numbers. How am I in the future? Who the fuck is Tyler?*

A small black rectangle buzzed on the table. It was somewhat smaller than a deck of

cards. Angela grabbed it and
turned it over.

"What the shit is this? A
tricorder?"

Angela turned the rectangle
over in her hands a few times.
She pushed the only button she
could see, and a screen clicked
on. It read:

Monday

August 11, 2014

9:23

And it had a picture of a
kitten behind all that.

"Jesus fucking Christ, I
gotta get out of here." Angela
stared at the IV tube going
into the back of her hand. She
didn't even want to rip the
tape off, let alone work the
needle out of her vein. She
heard noise coming from outside
the door, and pretended to be
asleep.

"Honey," the lawyer said. "The doctor is here."

Angela stopped pretending to sleep and started pretending to wake up.

Dr. Stephens began to speak. "We got some time with the MR machine in a little bit. These've been around for a long time now, but they're still a little scary to some people. It is completely safe and non-invasive. Here's what going to happen, okay? We're going to bring you into the room with the machine. We put you on the machine's table. It's really comfortable. It's like a bed. You get to wear headphones-"

Panic.

"-even listen to music if you want. The table lifts you up and then we put a helmet on you. It's a big helmet that goes over the headphones. It's not going to squish your head or anything like that. It looks kind of like a Stormtrooper helmet. The table slides back into what looks like a giant pipe."

Panic.

"It's open on both ends and nothing is going to spin or touch you or trap you or anything like that. The machine is going to use magnets to take pictures of your brain. We just want to make sure you don't have any bleeding there and that everything is getting enough oxygen. Okay? Two things though."

Panic.

"First, you can't move around in the machine. The pictures get blurry then. It's like an old-fashioned photograph, where you need to be still for it to turn out. You'll have the headphones to listen to, and there is a mirror so you can look around without moving your head. The second thing is that it is really loud in there. That's another reason why we give you the headphones. I just had to do this with an eight-year-old, and she told me that it sounded like chirpy birds with jackhammers. Okay? So, just be prepared."

"Chirpy birds?" Angela repeated the only words she remembered Dr. Stephens saying.

"Chirpy birds," Dr. Stephens smiled.

"All right," Angela said. What else could she say? Maybe the machine could tell why she was in the wrong body. Maybe this sort of thing happens in the future.

"Don't be afraid. We'll take care of you," the doctor said as she walked out of the room.

Angela wanted more than anything to hide.

But instead of hiding, people would be looking inside her brain.

She tried to clear her mind, and process everything that was happening. She retraced her steps to see where everything went wrong. Then if she got a time machine, she could go back and make the necessary changes.

The lawyer grabbed Angela's ankle and said, "Just tough it out, honey. We'll get through this." It was then that Angela saw the sticker on the lawyer's blazer. Angela squinted and saw that it was a visitor's pass. The name Susan Clark was scribbled on it. She wasn't a lawyer at all. This woman was Tyler's mom.

MINUS THREE

"*The Phantom Menace* was so
messed up, but I still don't
know how to feel about it,"
Robert said as he squeezed a
lemon wedge into his water
goblet. "I saw it three times,
and I'm pretty sure it's
terrible, but I want to watch
it when it comes out on video
just to be sure."

"It's no good, Robert."
Cliff explained, "There's no
Luke Skywalker to root for and
there's no bad guy to root
against. They messed up the
force. It's just no damned
good."

"I don't know. You can root
for, uh, Qui-gon, I guess. What
do you think, Angela?"

"Huh?" Angela had spaced out
for a moment, concentrating on
her menu options. She didn't
know why she ended up with
88

these guys, but her grandpa
always taught her the value of
free food. Plus, she found
Robert very attractive. She
found Cliff to be a big weirdo,
which was nearly equally
intriguing.

She rewound their
conversation a bit in her head,
before answering, "I've never
seen *Star Wars*."

"What do you mean?" Cliff
asked.

"No *Star Wars*?" Robert added
incredulously.

"Um, I saw one of the Ewok
things. I've watched some *Trek*.
I think I've seen every 'Deep
Space Nine.'"

"What you are saying doesn't
make any sense."

A waiter in a tuxedo shirt
and vest interrupted the
conversation and told the three
about today's specials. Angela
stopped listening after he took
too long describing the soup of

the day. Cliff was about to order when Robert stopped him.

"I'm sorry guys; I need a minute." Robert started frantically studying his menu.

Cliff asked the server for a cup of coffee and ordered a fried clam appetizer special for the table. After the waiter left, Cliff stacked his menu on top of Angela's.

"Every DS9, huh? That's commitment."

Angela smiled and fiddled with the locket around her neck. "Naw, it's just some neuroses and a blatant disregard for a social life. You would not believe the amount of time I've wasted watching TV. I don't like missing episodes, and I need to watch them in order. One of my local channels started showing 'Bewitched' at two in the morning, and I would tape every episode during the week and watch them all on Sunday morning."

"Hold up," Cliff interrupted. "You are watching a show about witchcraft instead of going to church? Pat Robertson was right all along. I bet you're one of them feminists who think all hetero sex is rape."

"Well, natch." The remark made Cliff smirk. "Actually," Angela said, "I went to Catholic school for years. We had a Friday mass. My dad said that counted, so we could skip on Sunday."

"So, he went to church without you?"

"Oh, god, no," Angela answered while playing with the white tablecloth.

"That special sounded good; monkfish with fennel, right? Is that what he said?" Robert asked this question and Angela made the noises of "I don't know" without opening her mouth or moving her tongue.

"Hold up, you're going to get fish? We're at a goddamned steakhouse!"

The waiter interrupted. "Have we decided?" He set a coffee in front of Cliff.

"Yes," Robert answered. He gestured to Angela in a movement that somehow said "ladies first."

Angela ordered a sixteen-ounce filet mignon cooked medium rare with steak fries. The waiter warned her that the steak was going to be "pretty red" and Angela shot him a look of contempt.

Cliff interrupted before it got ugly and requested, "the big porterhouse, rare, baked potato, crumbly bleu cheese on both. Oh, and I am quite aware that the rare steak might be cold in the middle."

Robert ordered his fish special, sauce on the side. He tried to balance the tone of his voice to sound apologetic about his friends to the waiter, but not so much so that Angela and Robert would catch on.

After the waiter left, Angela gave a half smile at Cliff. "What, I get the one-pound steak, so you got to get the two-pound steak? Masculinity threatened?"

"Madame, I represent the great state of Texas. No Yankee, regardless of the shape of their genitals, is going to eat more steak than me. You're just lucky you didn't order your steak medium well, or I'd've asked you to leave."

"When you gonna ask Robert to leave?"

"You're from Texas?" Robert asked. "You don't sound like you're from Texas."

"Yes, he does." Angela chimed in, "Texas is a big state with a lot of different accents."

"Question my Texasness, will you? I'll have you know that I am so Texas that I own multiple belt buckles and even a pair of spurs. They yell at me when I wear the spurs on campus as it messes up the, uh, sandstone."

"It's limestone," corrected Angela.

"Well, okay how about this? You know who taught my aunt to drive? This will tell you how Texas I am."

"Who?"

"No guesses"

"John Wayne." Robert guessed.

"John Wayne is from Iowa," Angela somehow remembered. She guessed, "Substitute teacher Peggy Hill?"

"Fictional, and from Montana."

"Jimmy Johnson?"

"You guys are terrible at this. Please stop." Cliff finished his coffee in one big gulp. "My aunt's driver's education teacher was none other than the Texas rattlesnake himself."

"Who is that?" Robert asked.

"Stone Cold Steve Austin."

"Bullshit," Angela responded.

"He had blonde hair and went by Steve Williams back then, but he taught my aunt to drive at Wharton County Junior College."

"Bullshit," Angela sang.

"God's honest truth! That's my big claim to fame. If I was gonna lie about it, it'd be a bigger lie. But my aunt really learned how to drive from Stone

Cold. I figure we all have something stupid like that."

"You're probably right." Robert conceded.

"I thought you were on a TV show?" Angela asked.

"Welp, I got more than one stupid claim to fame then." Cliff took a drink from the empty coffee mug, tonguing out the last drip of coffee.

"Robert, name your stupid thing." Angela commanded.

Robert's face pinched in for a moment before he said, "I can sing the periodic table of elements to the tune of 'Ten Little Indians'."

"The whole thing?" Cliff was impressed.

"Well, if the list is in front of me."

"How far without?"

"It kinda falls apart after Rutherfordium, but I can finish the actinides."

"So, your skill is knowing chemistry," Angela grinned, "and Cliff's skill is having an aunt?"

"Hold up. What's your skill then?" Cliff demanded.

Angela thought about this for a moment. An older waiter put a platter of fried clams and three bread and butter plates on the middle of the table. After he left, Angela answered, "I can tell you the job of any sitcom dad."

"That's kind of amazing," said Robert.

"Well, when in doubt, just say architect. Lots of TV show people are architects. Mike Brady: architect. And if you say Steve Douglas on 'My Three Sons' was an architect, most people will agree, when really, he was an aeronautical engineer. But, if you do get called on that, you could just say that he was an airplane architect."

"So, your skill is bullshitting?" asked Cliff, attempting to clarify.

"It's only about twenty percent bullshit. That's about as good as life gets," Angela explained.

Robert chuckled.

"All right," Cliff challenged, "what about 'Step by Step' dad, Patrick Duffy?"

"Not an architect, he was a self-employed contractor, worked with a lot of blueprints made by *architects*."

"What about 'ALF?'" wondered Robert.

"I never liked 'ALF.' My family watched 'MacGyver.'"

"Ah ha!"

"But the dad was a social worker, which would be a weird job for a show if it were not from the '80s. I feel like white people were always trying to make the world a better place on '80s TV shows. Now they just hang out and bang each other. Both have their merits, I guess." Angela grabbed a clam.

"That's fair."

"What about 'Webster?'" Cliff asked, using the fried clam as a shovel for cocktail sauce.

"I never hung out with Webster. I tried to go down on him, but I couldn't go that far down."

"Stop it," Robert requested.

Cliff turned to Robert. "I told you she was a sex pervert."

"The adopted dad and Webster's real dad were both football players."

"Webster was adopted?"

"My liberal friend Robert doesn't see color," Cliff announced.

After a few minutes of discussing the finer points of "Webster" versus "Diff'rent Strokes", the waiter came by with their food. They ate quietly for quite some time.

Eventually Robert spoke up, remarking about how quiet means that the food must be good.

"Or," Angela said munching on a fry, "You all are out of questions for me."

Cliff held a finger up at that remark and labored to finish the too large a bite of steak in his mouth. "I've got one more question: what's with the locket?"

Angela was caught off guard. She didn't want to talk about the locket. "It's private."

"Oh, come on. You make jokes about going down on a midget, but won't talk about your necklace."

"Pretty much." Angela chomped on a steak fry.

"She doesn't want to talk about it now, Cliff. Leave her be. We're having a nice night. We're eating nice food. Just drop it."

Cliff waved off Robert's nagging, and leaned closer to Angela. "I will literally answer any personal question you ask me. I mean, now, I have to know."

"She doesn't want to talk about it, Cliff."

"Any personal question?" Angela asked.

"I am a goddamned open book."

"All right, here's how this is going to work. You get to

101

ask one question about the locket with no follow ups."

"Okay. I've got to make it count."

"Yeah."

"All right." Cliff stopped and thought about which question would be best to ask. "Who is in the locket?" He was unhappy with his wording as soon as it came out. He had told too many jokes about genies' lamps to be so loose with the wording of such a thing. Angela could say nobody, because nobody would fit inside the necklace.

But then she answered.

"Penny."

Robert asked, "Wait. An actual penny or like a girl named Penny?"

"No follow-ups." Cliff responded. He had to respect the rules of the game.

"Well, you agreed to that. I want to know if she has a sister, girlfriend, or dog named Penny or a one cent piece."

Angela cut her steak into small bites and started eating again. She smiled.

"Why would she have a penny in her locket, Robert?"

"Maybe it's a lucky penny? The first penny she ever made?"

"You think Angela has the first penny she ever made? Even Scrooge McDuck waited until he made his first dime. Do you think she made her first penny sweeping out chimneys in Victorian England?"

"The number one dime, I forgot about that. It was like magical, right?"

"Naw, he was just being sentimental," Cliff disagreed.

"But that witch duck with
the black hair always wanted to
steal it."

"Well, Magica DeSpell
thought it was lucky," Angela
pointed out.

"Magica DeSpell!" Robert
celebrated. "So, wait, was the
dime powered by belief? Like a
cross against a vampire?"

"Wait, what?" Angela asked.

"You have to have to have
faith in order for a crucifix
to work against a vampire,"
Robert explained. "At least
that's how it works in *Fright
Night*."

"That's how it worked when
the X-men fought Dracula,"
Cliff added.

"Some things have meaning
just because people believe
they have meaning," Robert
declared.

"Doesn't that just make having meaning meaningless?" Angela wondered.

Robert said, "Well, you're looking at it backwards. Well, I mean, okay, that sounded harsh. Cliff, do you know what I mean?"

"Don't look at me, boss. I support returning to the gold standard."

The topics of conversation were lighter as they finished their main courses. They ordered dessert. Angela waited until it came out to get her compensation from Cliff.

"Well, Cliff you owe me a personal question."

"Sure do. Shoot."

"Why did you take us out?"

"To this restaurant? Steak."

"No, why us? Why arbitrarily decide that a shared birthday is justification for spending a hundred bucks or so on strangers?"

"All right. I said I'd answer. I'll answer." Cliff paused, as if trying to build drama. "My friends all either moved out of housing, graduated or transferred. I was worried that this year, I'd get, you know-"

"Lonely." offered Robert.

"Bored." Cliff corrected. "I don't know man. Robert seemed to like me, which is really most of what I'm looking for in a relationship. And you, Angela, I thought you were-"

"Yes?"

"Well, you know. . ." Cliff trailed off.

"What do I know?" Angela asked.

"A big Dave Foley fan, like me."

THREE

Angela cooperated with the
doctors and procedures as best
as she could. The MRI was noisy
and unsettling. It felt like
being buried alive in a
spaceship. The headphones
played some music from some
artist she didn't know, singing
over-produced songs about
feeling like a bag and having
the eye of the tiger, but not
in that Survivor way.

Hours later, she met with
Dr. Kassir from neurology. That
was trickier. Angela wanted to
lie and answer all his
questions as Tyler. If
everything was suddenly
"normal", she could get out of
here and figure out what the
hell is going on.

But in the end, she decided
to answer as honestly as
possible. What if she were

crazy? What if Tyler is brain damaged? Maybe this was something doctors in the future deal with? She guessed "no it wasn't" but had seen enough sitcoms to know the dangers of an elaborate lie. She didn't want any more zaniness in her life.

Mostly, she was worn out and desperately wanted to go home. She hoped that going home was somehow an option.

For his part, Dr. Kassir seemed like a perfectly personable guy with a list of questions that he had to make sound like a conversation and who would rather be anywhere else doing anything else.

He asked, "When were you born?"

Angela was sick of doctors, sick of being on display and sick of personal questions. "When I was just a little baby."

Dr. Kassir wrote some notes down, showing no reaction.

"I'm sorry," Angela apologized. "This is weird. July. I was born on July third, nineteen eighty-one. Tyler was born nine thirteen ninety-six. But I cheated for that answer," she said pointing to the hospital bracelet.

"Why is this weird?" the doctor asked without looking up.

"Seriously? I told you that my last memory before waking up in the hospital was from ten years ago? And that in all my other memories, I'm a lady? I'd kind of like to get back to my own body. I'd really like to do that." What was this guy's problem? Angela rubber both her eyes with her left hand. "Hopefully, my body isn't at the bottom of MacArthur Bay. It's kind of important to me. So, yeah, it's a little fucking weird!" Angela felt squeezed by sudden panic.

110

"Do you have any headaches, nausea?" Dr. Kassir had wavy brown hair, wire rimmed glasses, and a clean shaven, punchable face. Angela started to hate him for being so damned unhelpful.

"I felt nauseated when I first woke up, but I'm fine. Relatively speaking, of course. I mean, there is a tiny goose egg on Tyler's head, but I'm pretty good otherwise." Angela paused. "Well, there is one thing."

"Yes?"

"Everything has been blurry." She hated to admit weakness to this guy. "I can kind of squint and make things, uh, unblurry, but-"

"Have you considered putting those on?" Dr. Kassir asked, pointing to a pair of glasses on the end table.

Angela followed his suggestion. "Well, doc, that

did the trick." She started to hate Dr. Kassir even more for being so damned helpful.

"Good," he said indifferently. "Now, I'm going to need you to take those off."

"Fine." She complied, sneering.

"Look straight ahead." He shined a penlight into Angela's eyes. Then put his face uncomfortably close to hers. She could smell hair product and corn chips. He held a finger up. "I want you to touch your nose." He demonstrated the motion as though his request were ambiguous.

Angela complied, unenthusiastically.

"Good." He held his index finger up in front of his body. "Now I want you to touch my finger."

Angela did that thing.

"Good. Now I want you to touch your right thumb to each of the fingers on your right hand, one after the other." He demonstrated this action, as well.

Angela mimicked this thing, but it felt awkward.

"Good. Now, the other hand."

That way felt easier, but she could feel the lingering pain from where the IV had been.

After that, Dr. Kassir poked and prodded Angela for another three minutes making sure that she could feel all the parts of Tyler's body. When he was satisfied with those results, he made her walk back and forth a few times, balance on one leg, and do a few other tricks from the world's most underwhelming circus. Tyler's body was a little clumsy, but didn't seem troubled with any of these requests.

"So, doc, did I pass?" Angela asked, hoping for any new information as to her predicament.

"Everything checks out. I'm going to recommend you get a psych consult before you are discharged." He started to leave.

Angela had to say something before he left the room. "Wait, what does that mean?"

Dr. Kassir leaned his body on the threshold, resting. "Somebody from the department-"

"No, I mean, what do you think is going on? Shooting star? Fortune cookie wish? Soul stone? Why am I here? Do you think Tyler is in my body? Why is this the future? I need some help here."

"I'm sorry." Dr. Kassir didn't sound sorry. "None of that is my field."

He didn't sound sorry.

He didn't sound sorry in the slightest.

He walked out the door.

"Well, who the fuck's field is it?"

Dr. Kassir was already down the hall and offered no answer.

Angela sat restlessly on the bed. She rubbed her neck and looked at the phone. She had to call somebody. If she could contact somebody, she could prove that she was Angela and that everything was fucked up. And then-

Well she didn't know what would happen then.

Shannon, she needed to call Shannon. Angela read over the instructions on the phone as to dialing an outside line. She closed her eyes and took three deep breaths before dialing Shannon's number.

A man voice on the other end answered "Hello."

"Hello?"

"*Magadang umaga.*"

"Is Shannon there?"

"*Hindi ko alam kung anong gusto mo.*"

"Oh. Okay. Um, sorry" was all Angela could say before hanging up. She pinched the bridge of her nose with her left hand, then decided to try her dad. The phone barely rang before a robotic feminine voice answered, "Sorry, the voice mail box of the number you are trying to reach has not been set up. This message will be repeated." She slammed the phone down. Why couldn't she reach her family? Maybe she was just a crazy person.

Angela felt her eyes grow wet, and rubbed her face with her left hand. She turned the hand over and stared at the bruise from the IV. She began to remember that horror movie

116

about a hand transplant Robert made her watch.

Robert!

Robert was the last person who saw her. He must've seen something. He might know what happened.

What the hell was she going to say?

Fuck.

Angela dialed Robert's number. It rang once.

Please.

Twice.

Please.

Three times.

Then, a familiar voice began, "You've reached Robert's voicemail. I can't -well you know all that. Leave a message. Or just text me. Seriously, what year is this? Just text me."

BEEP

"Robert this is going to
sound weird, I'm probably going
to sound weird, but this is
Angela Brooks. We need to talk,
um, about the lighthouse. You
know, from, I guess, um, ten
years ago. Just give me a call
when you can. I don't know what
any my numbers are, or where I
live." She laughed. "I guess
I'll have to call you back."

Angela started making a
sound halfway between a chuckle
and a sob. Maybe she needed
that psych consult.

No!

Robert was real. She had
dialed his number and heard his
voice. She was not delusional.

Unless the voicemail was
also a delusion.

Angela tried to think her
way out of her problems, and
her frustrations blossomed.

She didn't even notice Ms. Clark come back into the room. She didn't notice Ms. Clark at all until Angela heard her asking, "Are you okay?"

"All things considered? I don't know. I'm sorry about all this."

Ms. Clark gave a look of concern. Angela put Tyler's glasses back on. "Look. I wear glasses now. That's a big change to deal with, huh?" She held her left hand over her face. "Big adjustment."

"You've worn glasses since the second grade, Tyler."

Angela stopped for a moment, and tried to regain her composure. "I'm sorry. You seem like a perfectly nice lady; I don't mean to make your life so weird. I'm sure this is the last thing you need to be dealing with." Angela sat up cross-legged on the bed. She closed her eyes and breathed deeply.

"Are you going to hurt yourself or anybody else?"

Angela drew a deep breath. "No."

Susan Clark touched Angela's ankle. "Would you like to get out of here?"

"Yeah."

"All right. I'm going to get you discharged." She said this very matter-of-factly, in that manner of speaking that only parents seem to be able to access.

"Really?"

"Just give me fifteen minutes."

"Wait. Why? Why are you helping me?"

Susan answered while leaving the room. "No matter what, you are still my son. It is still my job to help you out."

"All right," Angela responded, not sure what she thought about that answer. "Thank you."

Fifteen minutes later, Angela was getting dressed in Tyler's clothes and ready to head out the door.

Angela had zoned out at the house meeting. She had just wanted to lay in her dorm room and watch her "NewsRadio" VHS. She had fit almost an entire season's worth of episodes on this tape by recording everything in SLP and pausing during the commercials.

Angela had tried to stay quiet when the RA came knocking, but he somehow knew she was in there.

"Gotta come out, Angela!" yelled the RA. "We're electing house officers tonight. If you don't vote, you can't complain! And I know you love complaining."

Our relationship is not yet at this level of familiar teasing, she thought while remaining quiet. Angela paused her tape, realizing that she should have done that before the RA started yelling. WNYX's Dave Nelson stood motionlessly sipping his coffee, frozen in time.

"Come on! You can wear pajama pants and there's Rice Krispie treats!"

"Ugh, fine," she said, turning off the VCR.

And so, Angela now found herself sitting silently in the corner, blanking out as people re-introduced themselves with terrible ice-breakers and improv warm-ups so they could vote on a bunch of bullshit positions that did a bunch of nonsense. Physically incapable of paying attention to such things, Angela instead was daydreaming about her bathtub. The dorms didn't have bathtubs. The dorms had showers and communal showers at that. She could really go for a nice long bath. The kind where you had to turn the water back on in the middle because it had grown too cold in the tub. She could picture that hot water flowing over her big toe. She'd push the toe up into the spigot, but only a bit having learned a valuable lesson from Laura Petrie. Maybe dad would fly her back home for Thanksgiving.

"Okay, so Jillian will be our house's website czarina." Angela had no idea how long the RA had been speaking. Oh well. "We have one position left to fill, and that is the Birthday Czar!"

"What the fuck is a birthday czar? What are you saying?" Angela came out of her daze to realize that she had said these things aloud.

The RA bubbled, "She lives and speaks!" In addition to living and speaking, Angela was quite adept at glowering. "Well, Angela, as I wrote in my email from this morning, the birthday czar, or czarina, is responsible for decorating the doors of his or her peers when those peers have birthdays."

124

"This is an elected position?"

"Yes. C'mon. Let's just finish and then everybody can eat Rice Krispie treats. Any nominations?"

Some tall, skinny kid raised his hand. He had a nice sweater on and Angela liked his face. "Can I nominate myself?"

"Yes."

"Okay, then, I nominate myself," the kid said, standing up and tugging his sweater down.

"I'll second that. Is anybody going to run against Bob?"

"He prefers Robert!" yelled a blonde kid who sat cross-legged on the floor. Angela didn't remember meeting him. He looked like those kids who played hackeysack in Angela's high school. She was pretty sure all of those kids were on drugs.

"Is anybody going to run against Robert? Going once? Going twice? Nope? Congratulations, Robert, democracy works and you are now a birthday czar." The RA handed Robert a sheet of typing paper. "Here's the birthday list. Don't let all that power go to your head."

Angela turned to the tiny Asian girl next to her. What was her name? Grace? "Do you even elect czars?"

"We just did, Angie," the girl said as though Angela hadn't just witnessed this event.

"It's Angela."

"Whatever," replied the girl who might have been named Grace.

"No, I mean, traditionally, are czars an elected position?"

A stocky upperclassman gracefully slid through the crowd at the door. "In most situations, Czars are appointed." He grabbed three Krispie treats, and slid out of the room.

"That was kinda amazing," she heard Robert say. Angela agreed and said as much to the cross-legged blond.

"He's a senior who still lives in the dorms. I don't get it," he replied.

The bearded boy next to him added, "And he's got money too! Go get an apartment, you know?"

"He's rich?"

"No. Well, he might be," the blond added. "He won one of those reality game shows over the summer."

"But enough about him, I don't think we've met. I'm David, my friend here is also named David, and actually, that kid we were just talking about is also, also named David."

"All right," Angela pondered aloud, "so, when in doubt I can just call any dude who lives here 'Dave' and I got a pretty good chance of being right?"

"A little under twenty percent," blond Dave concluded. "It's one of the ways that the gods of housing amuse themselves."

"Fear the gods of housing and keep their commandments, for this is the duty of all of dorm life!" declared bearded Dave.

Angela smiled and nodded. She was trying to remember the words to that song from "The Kids in the Hall" about all the Daves.

"So," blond Dave asked, "did the freshman go to that park with the caverns again this year?"

Angela shrugged. "I dunno. House was pretty empty on Saturday. They all could've been there." Angela saw an opening in the crowd, and made her way towards the Krispie treats. Robert was asking the RA about summer birthdays, so Angela saw her opportunity. She snatched the third to last one and headed out the door. The RA hadn't even noticed her; he was too busy telling Robert that he could use his discretion when celebrating summer birthdays.

Within minutes, Angela was back to her room. The light was blinking on her cheap black answering machine. She pushed the button and listened. "Hey, it's just me. It's a little quiet over here, and I thought I'd check in on you. How's school going? Have classes started yet? Well, you know the drill, little sis, I'm here if you need me."

"I'm fine, everything's fine, ugh," replied Angela to the rounded square of black plastic.

She flopped on the bed and turned her VCR back on.

"Your last name is Garrelli?" said the TV.

KNOCK KNOCK KNOCK.

"Goddamnit."

Angela paused the tape and went to her door. She opened the door a third of the way and saw birthday czar Robert there with stocky senior Dave.

"What, do you need me to elect the Breakfast Big Wig? Surprise Party Kingpin? Boardgame Top Brass? The Guru of. . ."

"Getting down?" suggested senior Dave. "Man, I am absolutely calling myself the guru of getting down."

"Guru of getting down?" Robert said these words, incapable of parsing their meaning in this order.

"Hold up." Senior Dave stopped for a second to consider his newly invented dormitory office. "Naw," he said, "that's more bacon than this pan can handle."

"What are you guys doing here?"

Robert answered, "Your birthday wasn't on the sheet."

"I don't celebrate my birthday."

"Jehovah's witness?"

"No, I'm just not a baby. Birthday parties are for little kids and for grownup assholes." It took Angela a moment to realize that she was talking to somebody who had volunteered to celebrate everybody's birthday. She added in a "no offense" as quickly as she could.

"Well, as-" senior Dave started to say as he placed a hand on Angela's shoulder.

"Please don't touch me."

"All right." He removed his hand, and held up the other for good measure.

Robert confessed, "So, I looked up your birthday in the portrait directory."

"Ugh." *Why was this taking so long? If they tracked down my birthday already, why are they bothering me?*

"We are all a bunch of Harrison Schmitts!" Dave proclaimed.

Angela was not expecting that response. "What?" was all she could muster.

"We all have birthdays on July the third," explained Robert. That explanation was not adequate.

"So?"

"So, I'm taking us all out for steaks on Friday," Dave declared. "It'll be our unbirthday party. It'll be goddamned Harrison Schmitt day up in this mug."

"Thanks, but I'm not really, uh-"

"Lady, I'm offering you free steak just because we all share a birthday with Harrison Schmitt."

"I don't know who that is."

"Twelfth man on the moon!"

"It's also Kurtwood Smith's birthday," Robert interjected. "He's that guy from *Robocop* who is the dad on 'That '70s Show' now."

"Oh, Red Forman." Angela could picture him.

"So, are you in?"

"I don't know, guys. I don't like celebrating my birthday. I don't really know you, and I don't know if I want to-"

"Hold up. Just think about it for a day or two. You don't

have to say yes, but just don't
say no right now. Okay?"

"All right. You're Dave and
Robert, right?"

"Yeah."

"David Clifton, at your
service. Everybody calls me
Cliff on account of all the
other Daves up in this sumbuck.
We all have our own hands, but
we come from different moms."

"What?" asked Robert.

"It's a 'Kids in the Hall'
thing."

FOUR

Angela stepped into Susan
Clark's car. Happy to be out of
the hospital but wary that
wherever they were headed, it
wouldn't be home.

Angela buckled her belt.
"Ms. Clark?"

Susan sighed, looking
uncomfortable at being referred
to as "Ms. Clark" by her son.
"Yes?"

"Did you happen to see a big
blue stone, possibly on a ring,
among Tyler's personal
effects?"

"No, dear." Susan turned on
the car, checked her mirrors,
and made slight adjustments to
various knobs and switches.

"How about a locket?"

"Pardon?" Susan asked. She
put her hand behind Angela's
headrest and craned her neck in

order to back the car out of the space.

"A locket. Did you see a locket or anything like that?"

"No, I saw nothing like that." She paused, going over a mental check list. "I've got your phone and your wallet and your keys and our old camcorder which you had for some reason. I've never seen you wear a ring, let alone a locket. You haven't even worn a watch since you were eight." Susan fed a beige machine a small ticket. The machine thanked her and lifted the gate. She checked both directions, and then slowly pulled out of the parking structure. "Why do you ask?"

Honesty was the best policy, right? "I think it might be the magic, body swapping MacGuffin. The ring with the blue stone, that is, not the locket. The locket has sentimental value." Angela stopped, afraid of Susan Clark's possible reaction to this news. Not finding any reaction at all, Angela continued speaking. "I know that it sounds very silly, but I feel as though the ring might be the key to all this. Maybe I find that, and you get your son back, and I go back to my shitty life in 2004."

"Please don't swear in my car, Tyler." Susan turned the radio onto a classical station and kept the volume low.

"My *crummy* life in 2004. I mean, it was crummy, but it was mine. You know?" Angela was starting to question Susan's focus on this situation.

"No, I do not know. I don't understand a thing about what is happening. Why do you think you are a girl? Is this some sort of defense mechanism?" The words tripped awkwardly from her mouth. "Did something happen to you, sexually? Do you feel like you were born in the wrong body? Are you thinking about transitioning?" Susan's

137

eyes darted left and right, as she nervously checked all her mirrors.

"Transitioning?"

"You know," Susan took a pause to gather strength, "like, um, taking hormones and living as a woman?" Susan shifted awkwardly in her seat.

"No." Angela grew louder. "No. I'm in the wrong body, but I wasn't born in the wrong body. I was born in the right one. As a girl. In Pittsburgh. In 1981." *Listen to the words I am saying, woman!*

"I'm going to ask you this once, and you need to answer me honestly." Susan steeled herself. Now she stared unblinkingly at the road. "Is this a joke?"

"What?"

"Is this some sort of joke that everybody is playing on me? Are there hidden cameras around? Is Allen Funt going to be making fun of me on TV?"

"No, ma'am. This is not a joke," Angela reassured Tyler's mom. "And I'm pretty sure Allen Funt died a couple of years ago. Well, I guess more than a couple of years ago, now." She chuckled at the absurdity of the situation. "Jesus, twenty fourteen. So, can you catch me up on things?"

"Please don't swear in my car."

Angela considering informing Susan about the differences between swearing and blasphemy, but presently had other hills upon which to die. Instead, she said, "I'll see what I can do about that. I've got a few other things on my mind. All right?"

"Fine. What do you want to know?"

She recognized Ms. Clark's tone as patronizing, but no

longer cared. "Shi-oot. I dunno. Um, are people 'transitioning' a lot? Is that a thing? Is that common now?"

"It isn't in my neighborhood. Although there is that one woman who works at the Target store, I think she might be. Or he. No, I'm supposed to say she because he dresses as a she. I mean because she dresses as a she."

"Um, are there still fifty states?"

"Of course."

"Well, don't say it like that. New York or California could have been broken up. We could have finally made Puerto Rico into a state. We could have annexed Ontario, for all I care."

"It's the same fifty states, Tyler."

Angela let that "Tyler" slide. "Who's the president?"

"Barack Obama."

"Are those words? What are you saying to me?"

"His first name is Barack. His last name is Obama. He's from Hawaii, he was a Senator for Illinois and then became our first black President."

"Black President, huh? Good for us."

"Actually, I think he's mixed."

"Oh."

"Is 'mixed' still okay to say?"

"I don't know."

"I know mulatto is bad, now, but I always thought it was a pretty word."

"I, uh, I don't know."

"What else do you have?" Susan asked. She was now somewhat cheerier.

"Um, I don't what else to ask. When did they end up canceling 'The Simpsons'?"

"I don't think they have."

"No shi-take mushrooms. Are the Rolling Stones still alive?

"I believe so. The main two guys are at least."

"Hmm. . . Well, I see this car isn't flying."

"No flying cars."

"Hoverboards?"

"Nope."

"Dehydrated pizza delivery?"

"No."

"Can you tell me who won the last ten Super Bowls in case I end up back in 2004?"

"I have no idea. You can just wiki it when we get home."

"What is wiki?"

"It's an online encyclopedia."

"Like Encarta?" asked Angela, whose mind was full of memories of CD-ROMs, Encyclopedia Britannica commercials, and Pueblo, Colorado 81009.

"Not quite like Encarta. It's, what do they call it? Open? Everybody can add to it or edit it, and they have entries on everything from Gilgamesh to. . . Chewbacca. That's the little green guy in *Star Wars*, right?"

"I don't do *Star Wars*."

"Well, I could look up if that is the name of the little green guy on Wikipedia."

"Oh."

"It's great. If you are watching an old movie, you can look it up and see who all the actors are, and what else they've done. Then you can fall down a rabbit hole and start reading one random thing after another. Sometimes things are stubs, so you can add more information to the article and help other people who are looking for things."

"So, in the future, you read and write encyclopedias for fun?"

"Don't make fun of me! You're the one that showed me all about this stuff!"

"I," Angela stopped. What could she do? *All right. When I get back to the Clarks' house, I'll try Robert again. Then Cliff. Actually, Cliff might be the person I know who is most likely to believe this crazy story. Jesus, he's probably researched six cases just like this. Cliff might know just what to do.*

"So, do we live around here?"

Susan sighed or possibly grunted. "Yes, Tyler, we do."

The car was quiet for a moment, with only the faint sounds of Handel's Water Music breaking the silence.

"So, do we have anything cool like a robot vacuum?"

"Actually. . ."

MINUS FIVE

Hey little sis,

I'm writing this from the
computer lab on campus. The RA
told me that I can print this
out, but I have no idea where.
I guess if you are getting
this, I figured it out. College
is going okay, and I've managed
to make it to every Spanish
class on time even though it
starts at 8:30 in the morning.

Okay, so I fall asleep in it
all the time. I'm not the only
one though. There's this huge
Nigerian guy who falls asleep
more than me, and he snores
with a nose whistle.

They are making me take a gym
class. Can you believe that? I
have to take a gym class-

IN COLLEGE.

[This guy Elliot says I can make that a different color before I print it. Be impressed if that works. If it doesn't, I am not going to try a second time.]

This semester's PE offerings were kind of gross. Weight training, running and ball room dancing. I was hoping for kickball, but instead I have a choice between my two least favorite things and having a bunch of weirdos rubbing up against my leg to a bunch of music by a bunch of dead guys. Thanks college! I'm sure that there will be plenty of situations in the future where the only way out will be to waltz.

You should be in school yourself when you get this. Let me know who you get for English this year. Research and Bob was a nightmare of suck for me, but

maybe you can do a paper on
Nick at Night or something.
Here's hoping you get Mrs. T
for History.

If dad picks me up, I'll be
home for thanksgiving. Maybe we
can cook dinner together or
something. Or maybe I can cook
dinner and you can watch your
robot show. (haha)

They say this machine can check
your spelling mistakes and
stuff, but I'm not sure how
that works, either. I'm still
impressed with the erase ribbon
on our typewriter. This is all
new Babylon 9 stuff for me.

Anyways, they told me that if I
hold down one of these buttons
and hit P it will print.

Fingers crossed.

Your big sis,

Shannon.

P.S. Join a damned club this
year you damned hermit. Or at
least go outside once in a
while. The sun is good for you.

FIVE

As soon as they got to the
Clarks' house, Angela asked to
use the phone.

Susan was quick to respond:
"Why don't you just use your
own phone?"

Angela was taken aback.
Tyler had his own line? Oh
wait, Susan mentioned something
about a cellphone. She was
about to ask about it, when
Susan handed her a rectangle.

"This is a phone?" Angela
did not think that this was a
dumb question.

"Yes, Tyler." Ms. Clark shot
Angela a sideways glance.
"Thankfully it wasn't damaged,
or you'd be paying for it."

"Do I have a bedroom?"
Angela did think that this was
a dumb question, but it was too
late to un-ask it.

"Oh, for the love of Pete!" Susan led Angela down a hallway and to a decent sized bedroom. Angela thought it was pretty clean for a teenage boy. The bed was made, there weren't any clothes on the floor, and nothing smelled like a gym locker. The biggest mess was an unruly pile of books near what Angela assumed was a computer. It had a keyboard, but it didn't have a tower and there was only one cord coming out of it. The mouse wasn't even tethered to the machine. Angela scanned the walls and saw a poster with something that kind of looked like Legos, and another poster that contained a still from that famous bigfoot sighting video.

Angela sat on the bed. She decided to try to call Cliff, first.

Now, she just had to figure out how to use the rectangle.

She pushed the button that had shown the date and a cat on

the other rectangle. It did the same thing on this one, only without the cat. There was a green monster in the background here, and it had a cube for a head. The foreground had a collection of tiny pictures and strange almost sentences.

"Matt Y and Asad A are tweeting about pound sign Aladdin?" She read these words aloud to see if it made any more sense.

It did not.

She pushed the button again and at various speeds, but nothing seemed to happen. It was then that Angela noticed a string of glowing letters towards the bottom of the screen that read, "slide to unlock".

What did that mean?

She slid the phone on the bed. Nothing. She tilted it. Nothing. She shook it. Nothing. She touched the screen to feel for more buttons, and everything moved. "Oh, a touchscreen. I'm so fucking dumb."

She slid her finger over the words to unlock the phone. "ENTER PASSCODE," the phone demanded. She tried 1-2-3-4, nope. 0-0-0-0, nope. "Jesus fucking Christ, I could've dialed on a rotary by now."

She came up with a new plan and left the room.

"Excuse me, Ms. Clark," Angela yelled from the hall.

"Yes, dear?" she answered, slightly annoyed.

"Um, what is the passcode to this phone?"

"Whatever you set it as Tyler."

"Yeah, um, look, I don't want to play this game." Angela walked down the hall toward the living room. "Can you just tell me the passcode to this phone?"

"I'm sorry, but I respect my son's privacy and I do not know the passcode to his phone." Ms. Clark sat on the couch and turned on the television. On the flat screen, two men were hanging drywall.

Angela looked at Susan.

"I really don't."

Angela raised an eyebrow.

"I'm telling you the truth."

Angela tilted her head.

"8487."

"Thank you."

Ms. Clark changed the channel to some show where an old lady was baking. Angela returned to Tyler's room. She slid to unlock, put in the passcode, and was greeted with 24 smaller squares. She whispered to herself, "Calendar, camera, maps, clock, Instant-gram, bird, ghost, picture of a telephone! Ha ha!"

She touched the picture of a telephone and saw a list of names. "Contacts. . . Keypad, here we go. Ha! I am smarter than this phone!"

Angela celebrated her accomplishments. She was getting the hang of the future. She pushed the screen's digits that corresponded to Cliff's telephone number. There was no feel to it, but at least it sounded like a touchtone phone. That was a good thing.

It wasn't ringing though.

She held it up to her ear to be sure.

Nope.

Damned thing doesn't work. Is there no signal in here?

Angela walked around the room in circles waving the phone about, before she deemed it necessary to leave Tyler's room again. "Ms. Clark?"

"Yes?" Her voice contained a little more annoyance this time.

She walked into the living room, holding the phone out in front of her. "Um, why isn't the phone ringing?"

"You have to push the little green phone," Ms. Clark said, before turning her attention back to the television, which was now showing a real estate agent leading a couple on a tour of a shed in which they hoped to live.

"I did that, Angela explained. "And then I went to keypad. And then I pushed in the numbers."

"You have to push the little green phone on this screen after you do that."

"Oh. Duh. I'm dumb, sorry."

"Don't call yourself dumb."

"Sorry." Angela felt suddenly guilty as though she

were insulting this woman's
child in front of her.

"Who are you calling?"

"A friend of mine named
Cliff. He knows a lot about
weird sh- weird stuff like
this. Well maybe not exactly
like this."

"You don't know anybody
named Cliff." Susan Clark
seemed confident in this
information.

"We went to college
together."

"Tyler, you haven't even-"

"Shh- it's ringing!"

"Don't shush me!"

Angela hurried back to
Tyler's room just as somebody
picked up on the other end.
"Jell-o."

"Cliff?"

"Yeah, what's up?"

"All right, so this is going to sound weird, but this is Angela."

"All right Angela, why is this weird?"

"This is Angela Brooks."

"Oh, I used to know an Angela Brooks."

"Yeah that's me," she tried to explain.

"I don't follow."

"All right, so remember about ten years ago with your stupid fucking plan about finding a stupid fucking diamond at that stupid fucking lighthouse."

"Course I do; it was a great plan."

"Asshole! I grabbed something in that fucking lighthouse, passed out, and when I wake up I'm some fucking teenage boy ten years into the future."

158

"Son, I don't know if what you're saying makes sense to you, but it doesn't make a damn lick of sense to me."

"No, no, none of it makes any sense." Angela decided to lay all her cards on the table. "But this is fucking Angela Brooks from 2004. As I understand it, it is now 2014 and I am in the body of some kid named Tyler Clark. I need to know what happened at the lighthouse, what happened to my body, and what the fuck I can do to get back in that body."

"This is more bacon than this pan can handle."

"What?"

"You're kind of hitting me with a lot of weird stuff right now," came the voice from the phone.

"Oh, am I?" Angela repressed the urge to yell, not wanting to deal with Susan's wrath. Still the words came out as a whispered scream. "I'm hitting you with a lot of weird stuff?" she raged. "This is all because of your fucking lighthouse. This is your fucking mess. I need you to fix it."

"What's the password?"

"Password?"

"Uh-huh, your all purposes contingency password. I gave one to you and one to Robert and one to Timothy."

One of the benefits of having a lunatic like Cliff for a friend is that he insisted on bizarre contingency plans. They had extensive conversations about what they would do in case of zombies, how to tip each other off if one of them is being kidnapped, an agreement to share any secret identities in case of super-powers, and codes for identification purposes in instances of doppelgangers, body snatchers and the like.

Angela experienced a unique blend of relief and annoyance. She let out a sharp breath. "For one thing, you didn't give us passwords. We each came up with our own password. It was on the second Kurtwood Smith day. Robert's was Arbogast, yours was Lascivious Crumb, and mine is Tubal-Cain. Timothy is part of the code that means I think you're full of bullshit because you were obsessed with that song from the seventies about cannibalism."

"It's Salacious Crumb. He's from *Star-*"

"Jesus fucking Christ, I don't give a shit about *Star Wars*! You asked for my password. Tubal-Cain, goddamnit!"

"Well, I'll be dipped in shit. This is. . . unexpected."

"Ya think?"

Silence.

"Cliff? Are you there?" Angela wondered into the phone.

"Hold up. Can we meet somewhere? I hate talking on the phone."

"Oh, you hate talking on the phone?"

"Yeah."

"Jesus fucking Christ! Fine. We can meet wherever you'd fucking like so long as you fix this." She was full on yelling now, no longer caring about the consequences. Yelling at Cliff made Angela feel more like herself than she had felt all that day.

"Where you at?"

"I have no idea. Hold on." She held her hand over the phone. "Ms. Clark! What's the address here?"

"Please don't yell across the house, Tyler."

"Hold on." Angela walked to the living room and politely re-stated her question to Ms. Clark.

She answered, "Thank you. The address is 1859 Compton avenue."

"1859 Compton."

"All right, I'm gonna Google that. Oh! I know right where that is."

"Great," Angela said. Her use of the word was not convincing.

"There's a coffee shop right by you. Head out your front door, turn left, and walk to Colton Street. It's about two blocks. From there you should be able to see a sign that reads 'Grounds for Appeal'. I can meet you there in about," he paused, "forty-five minutes?"

"Forty-five minutes?" she asked for confirmation.

"Forty-five minutes, give or take."

"All right. I'll look for you. I don't remember what I look like well enough to tell you what I look like."

"It says you're on an iPhone. You can just take a picture and send it to me. Or we can Facetime."

It was hard enough just figuring out how to call. Angela responded, "Look, I'll just meet you in forty-five minutes. I'll be the one drinking all the coffee."

"All right. See you then." The phone beeped, and Angela shoved it into her pocket. She found a hoodie in the closet and tossed it on.

As she walked towards the front door of the house, Ms. Clark asked, "Where are you going?"

"Out."

"When are you coming back?"

"Me? Hopefully never. This body? Sometime later."

"That isn't funny," Ms. Clark flatly stated.

"You sure? I think it is fucking hilarious, Susan. A laugh fucking riot." Angela slammed the door behind herself.

From behind the door, Angela heard, "That is not acceptable behavior, young man. I am going to count to three."

Angela rolled her eyes and began walking. After three steps, she stopped and realized that she had no purse, no wallet, and no money.

"Tyler Austin Clark!" came the voice from the other side of the door.

She turned around and walked back, standing outside the threshold, frozen.

"Get back in here, right now."

A pause.

"So, help me!" the voice continued.

It might have been a full minute before she started walking away again. Angela turned left and headed towards Colton Street. She passed by a group of teenagers taking turns playing on a single skateboard; it didn't hover.

This future was bullshit.

She stepped off the sidewalk to allow a dad pushing a stroller to get past.

Nobody was looking at her. Nobody was acknowledging this freak situation. They couldn't tell. Angela towered over an old woman waiting for the light

to change at a crosswalk. How
tall was Tyler, anyway?

She walked past a young,
African American woman with a
shaved head, and then caught a
man stopping mid-stride to
check that woman out. "That's
when you know a girl is good-
looking," he said to Angela,
"when she looks good bald-
headed. You know what I'm
saying?"

Angela nodded awkwardly,
knowing only some of what he
was saying.

Shannon stood on the short green carpeting in the hallway, outside her little sister's door. She stopped to look at the pictures on the wall. Her mom liked to buy these giant frames that held half a dozen photos in a pseudo-collage style. Shannon was particularly drawn to a Polaroid of Angela and herself. She was maybe six and Angela was probably three. They were dressed alike in these white long sleeve shirts and these awful pink corduroy overalls. She was giving Angela bunny ears and Angela was smiling like a doofus.

Was she too mean? Was she a bad sister?

Shannon tried to think of all the times she did something nice for Angela, and all the times she helped her. She was having trouble thinking of anything big, anything that seemed to mean anything.

Shannon was still in her church clothes with her curly brown hair pulled back sloppily. Two relatives had called her a young woman and told her that she looked older than fifteen. Shannon briefly smiled at the idea that the only way she could make herself look more mature was by wearing the dowdy church clothes she hated. What had her mom called things like that? Catch twenty-fours?

Could she become a good sister now, after twelve years of being terrible? Would she have to be good for twelve years to break even? Even so, she'd have to try.

Shannon held the necklace in her right hand, rolling the chain around her palm feeling hundreds of small vibrations. She practiced some phrases in her head before reaching for the door knob.

She pulled back. It could wait until tomorrow. It could wait until next week. Hell, it could wait for another year.

No. *Just do it now,* she thought. *Do it now, so you can move on to the next thing.* Why did she feel butterflies over this? Why was talking to her little sister at all intimidating? She grabbed the door knob.

Locked.

She *could* do this tomorrow. She could do this next week. She could do this next year.

She knocked.

"Angela? Can you open the door?"

There was no reply. Shannon stared down at the patterns in the strange green carpet of their hallway. She had never noticed how odd it looked. It looked like clouds, like brains, like lumpy oatmeal.

"Angela. . ." Shannon sang the name.

No reply.

Shannon turned and walked down the hall toward her own room. She tried. No one could say that she didn't try.

She stopped.

No.

Shannon turned the other way, and headed toward the kitchen. She went over to the kitchen counter and grabbed a quarter out of a cloudy green ashtray full of change. The quarter was worn and had a black sticky residue on it. It was one of those ones with a drummer on the back instead of an eagle.

Shannon walked down the hall carrying the coin as though it were a hotel key. She came back to Angela's threshold and said, "You've lost your last chance. Ready or not, I'm unlocking your door."

Shannon stuck the quarter in the keyhole, well more key slot, and turned it. She opened the door to find Angela lying face up on her bed, staring at the ceiling. Shannon looked up too, just to spot check for any anomalies. She found only the standard bumps and sparkles.

"Are you doing okay?" She took a seat by her little sister's feet.

Angela kept staring at the ceiling, her eyelids twitching slightly around her big, bloodshot eyes.

Shannon touched Angela's shin. "Hey, um, I'm really sorry that I missed your birthday party." She kept her hand on her sister's leg, waiting for a response.

"I don't care," Angela finally said.

A faint smile came across Shannon's lips. "Well, I still should have been there."

"It doesn't matter." Angela replied, and Shannon's smile faded.

"Hey, listen to me. I'm your sister. I'm here for you. From now on, I'm always going to be here for you." Shannon's face turned red at the last line, and she started blinking quickly. Her eyes darted around the room, then back to her sister, and then finally back to her hand. She got up off the bed.

"I think you should have this." Shannon held her hand out to Angela. She took a step toward her sister before Angela stopped staring at the ceiling and sat up.

Angela looked at her sister's hand, then looked at her sister. She couldn't look Shannon in the eyes, instead it appeared as though she were counting the freckles on her big sister's nose.

Angela took the necklace from Shannon and stared at the round trinket attached to the chain.

"Go ahead," the big sister said.

Angela opened the locket and saw the penny.

SIX

The coffee shop was easy
enough to find, though its
signage and décor struck Angela
as austere. It had about a
dozen small tables with wire
chairs scattered around them.
She studied the menu for a bit
before she remembered that she
had no purse, no wallet and no
money. She fumbled through her
pockets on the off chance of
finding any cash but was
luckless.

"I'm, uh, just meeting
somebody here," Angela said to
the barista. She awkwardly
pointed down on the word
'here'.

"That's great. There's
plenty of room, don't worry."
The barista was right. Only two
tables were occupied. One was
being used by a man with a
laptop computer. At the other
table were two twenty-
somethings sitting intimately

close, but staring away from each other, each down into her hands. As Angela walked to a table, the barista yelled to her, "So Tyler, hot date?"

Angela chuckled awkwardly.

She made her way to a table, and sat. Angela figured that it took about 10 minutes to walk here, so she had about thirty-five more minutes to kill. She scanned the coffee shop for a television.

Nothing.

She looked around the coffee shop for a magazine.

Nothing.

She looked by the front door, where she could usually find a stack of free newspapers. You know the kind, the ones that were full of ads for escort services toward the back.

Not even that.

Angela was alone with her thoughts, which was the last thing she wanted right now. So, she sat in an uncomfortable wire chair and tried to clear her thoughts.

Mostly unsuccessfully.

She had been waiting for nearly half an hour before Cliff walked in. She spotted him right away. He hadn't changed much, a little heavier in beard and in body. With growing anxiety in her gut, she flagged him down.

"Cliff!"

"Hey, uh, you. You want a coffee?"

She walked over to him. "Thanks, yeah. I didn't bring any money."

"Some things never change."

She punched him and called him a dick. "Well, shit, maybe it is you." He ordered two large coffees in "for-here cups". The barista handed him two large mugs. Cliff passed one off to Angela, and then headed to the coffee bar where he grabbed a Sweet and Low. He carefully poured half the pink package into his cup, threw the rest away.

Cliff took a sip of the coffee. "Should have tasted it first. Didn't need the sweetener."

"You seem pretty even-keeled for a guy who just got told this crazy story," Angela stated.

"Do I seem nonplussed to you?"

"No. Nonplussed means confused or bewildered. You seem non-nonplussed."

"Uh-huh," Cliff began, "it's not like I can really believe your batshit story."

"I gave you the pass- Why the fuck did you even want to

meet me if you didn't believe me?"

"I thought I might be on a hidden camera show. I've always wanted Tracy Morgan to introduce me." He walked to a table in the corner. "Being on TV is worth the price of a cup of coffee."

"TV?"

"Uh-huh. My old game show clip has about three hundred thousand YouTube views. I don't know about this one, though. Maybe next time come up with a prank that is less, um, impossible." He sipped the coffee. "I hate these mugs."

"You motherfucker! All the shit I've heard from you over the years? Your Kennedy theories, your bullshit spoon-bending parties, the fucking alien cover-ups, and now you're saying a soul swap is impossible!"

"Your information is a little dated. I stopped believing in all that stuff almost ten years ago. Heck, I don't even believe in souls, let alone this soul-swapping malarkey."

"I gave you the all-purpose password."

"Uh-huh."

"Ask me something else. Anything. Look, I'm not wearing an ear piece. Nobody is around to feed me answers."

"Kid," Cliff said dismissively, "nothing I ask you is going to make the situation less impossible."

Angela pushed her glasses up slightly and pinched the bridge of her nose with her left thumb and index finger. She chuckled. Cliff watched these movements and raised an eyebrow ever so slightly.

"You're pretty good," he remarked.

"Isn't there some quote you used to say about-"

"Arthur Conan Doyle said you rule out the impossible, and whatever improbable thing is left is the truth. Problem is, one, you are in the former category, and, two, Mr. Doyle believed in fairies."

"Not that one, the thing with Ray Bradbury and technology being magic to cavemen or something, something."

"It was Arthur C. Clarke. Something like, you can't distinguish a big old advance in technology from magic. But you're not giving me advanced technology; you're talking to me about a magic lighthouse."

Both Arthur Cs were of no use to Angela.

"It might have been the ring," she posited. "I really don't know what it was."

"Well, it's not the ring; you guys didn't find the ring." Cliff took a swig of coffee. "It turned up in Sweden in oh-eight."

"If it wasn't the ring, maybe it *does* have something to do with the lighthouse."

"Or maybe, just maybe, it's a bunch of bullshit."

"Fine. You know what? Fine. Don't help me. You're not going to be on TV. Just leave and do whatever the fuck you want!"

Cliff got up and started to leave. Angela stopped him.

"Wait. I didn't- Can you just sit with me and drink this coffee with me? I'm sorry. I mean, I'm hella-pissed at you, and you're an asshole and all, but I need like five minutes of a familiar face before I go nuts. I know everybody thinks I'm nuts, but, well, maybe," She trailed off. "It would just be easier to be nuts."

Cliff turned around. "I didn't accuse you of being crazy. I accused you of being a liar."

"Well there's that."

"Well, I got this coffee in this stupid for-here mug. Might as well finish it." He sat back down. "And, hell, I don't get a lot of requests from people to look at this damn face."

Angela smiled, but felt like crying. She took a long sip of coffee before speaking. "The beard really came in. It was patchy before."

"Yeah."

Angela closed her eyes and leaned her head back. She let out two short, sharp breaths. "Have you had a chance to say, 'No, the beard stays! You go!' to anybody?"

"What?" Cliff's eyebrow went higher this time.

"You know, like in that 'Kids in the Hall' bit?"

"I say that at least twice a month."

Angela and Cliff each took a long drink of coffee. He squinted and looked into her eyes long enough to make her uncomfortable.

Well, more uncomfortable.

"Just after we met during O-week, I took us to Pizza Castle. What did I buy you there?"

"First off, you were three years ahead of me. We didn't meet during O-week. We met at the first house meeting."

"Uh huh."

"Second off, I had a bad experience at Pizza Castle before, Cliff. I don't go to Pizza Castle. You took us out for steaks. I don't remember what you got, something Texas-sized probably. I might've had filet. I usually go for filet. Oh, and fucking Robert got fish, because he is so wrong."

Cliff was not expecting that answer. This boy wasn't wearing an earpiece, and that wasn't the sort of question one would prep for on a prank show. He didn't know what to do for a full two minutes.

And so, they both sat quietly, holding the handles of their coffee mugs with their left hands, slowly sipping their coffees, as some slightly jazzy, acoustic cover of a popular song played softly over the sounds of milk steaming and computer keys clicking.

Maybe this was Angela, somehow.

Cliff devised one last test. "What did the dad do on *"Mr. Belvedere"*?

"His name was George, he was Bob Uecker and he was a sportswriter who then became a sportscaster." There was a pause and a smile. "He was not an architect."

"Holy shit." Cliff chuckled.

"Yeah."

"Holy shit. So, this is a little crazy. Should we go to a scientist or something?"

"I was already in the hospital. They took pictures of my brain, or Tyler's brain. Whatever. I don't know whose brain it is. I guess it looked normal. What sort of scientist would you recommend?"

"One in a very clean white lab coat and tesla coils in the background."

"Is that a joke?"

"Best I can attempt in this situation, darlin'. Explain to me what exactly happened."

"I don't know what happened. That's why I'm talking to you."

"But, no, no, no. What do you remember?" Cliff leaned forward in his chair.

"I went out to the lighthouse with Robert. He was talking some shit about movies. We broke into the lighthouse. We found a stone with 1911 on it. I smashed a hole in the wall, reached in, and next thing I know I wake up in a hospital in 2014 as some kid named Tyler."

"Do you remember between the lighthouse and the hospital?"

"No."

"Do you have any of Tyler's memories?"

"I don't think so. I didn't recognize his mom. I didn't recognize his house or his room. I don't know how to use his phone."

"Hmm." Cliff leaned back in his seat.

"That's the best you got? Hmm?"

"Well, was Tyler at the lighthouse? How did Tyler end up in the hospital?"

"Huh. I kind of assumed he went to the lighthouse. I don't really know. I didn't ask."

"Do you have Tyler's phone? Is there any chance that he is trying to call you?"

"Here," she said, handing him the phone. "The passcode is, um, shit. . . eighteen fifty-nine? No that was the address. Shit." Angela massaged her temples.

"Who is this Hannah who keeps texting you?"

"How the shit should I know? Try eighty-four eighty-seven."

The phone clicked. "Okay. That worked. Seriously, she's texted you like twenty times."

"Is she talking about body swapping spells or anything like that?"

"Nope. 'Where are you', 'what's going on', emoji, emoji-"

"Then I don't care."

"Okay. I'm going to go through your, his, social media and emails and shit."

"All right."

Angela sat quietly and listened to the clicking of the phone, the lightly playing acoustic rock of the coffee shop, and occasionally sounds from the steam wand foaming milk.

"So, what you been up to?"

"How do you mean?" Angela wondered.

"What have you been doing in this body? What's it like? I've only had this one since about age sixteen, and it just keeps on getting fatter and hairier."

"Well, it's weird," Angela admitted. "It's weird being taller."

"That's the weird part?"

"I mean, sure. There's other bits too."

"Yeah, the bits. You, uh, try out the new equipment?"

"Gross."

"It's a once in a lifetime opportunity, one would think."

"My first experience with having a penis was having a catheter removed."

"Yuck."

"Yeah. And even if I wanted to do anything salacious or lascivious, his mom has been next to me this whole time. What I'm saying is that nothing terribly arousing has occurred."

Cliff smirked. "Are you sure that this Tyler kid is a teenaged boy?"

"That's the thing, too! I don't want to touch some seventeen-year-old kid's junk. It seems molester-y."

"Well. . ."

"Molestery," Angela declared.

"Fair enough."

"For the most part I don't know whether to, what's your expression? Crap or wind my watch?"

"That's the one." The phone blooped. "Oh good, it's Hannah again."

"I don't know man. She must be the girlfriend. I guess I did see that name kept on popping up in different colored, uh, boxes on the phone's," she tried to figure out the proper word and settled on, "display."

"You are gonna get Tyler in so much trouble; you haven't checked in and Hannah is freaking out. On top of the texts, she'd tweeted at you, facebooked, snap-chatted-"

"Look-"

"She is one thirsty-"

"Look, I'm ducking this kid's friends. I'm not going to waste time getting into wacky situations where I have to pretend to know how to waterski or something. I just want to go home."

"Wacky situations are what make life worth living, darlin'. You got no plans of getting into a bar fight or sexing up a lady or any of the other usually hypothetical 'what would you do?' type of situations?" Cliff continued staring at Tyler's phone while talking to Angela. She hoped that it meant that he was making progress.

"Cliff, you went to college with me."

"Uh-huh."

"I've already done all that shit."

"Fair enough," he replied, smiling.

Angela squirmed and stretched in her chair. "This is boring. Did you find anything useful yet? Or is it all Hannah?"

"Meh."

Angela sighed. "I did pee standing up after the catheter was out. It was disastrous. There was blood in it and the stream went in two directions."

"That happens sometimes."

"Blood?"

"No, the stream thing. Sometimes there is like a little fuzz ball from my underpants in the end of the cock hole and it shoots out in all directions."

"Ew."

"Or after you fuck."

"Boys are gross."

"Yep."

"Hey Cliff?"

"Uh-huh."

"What happened to me?"

"I'm still looking."

"No," Angela specified, "I mean, my body, after the lighthouse."

"Hold up, I've got something," Cliff said, happy to change topics.

"Do you know where the blue diamond is?"

"No," Cliff replied, having to think about the question for a bit. He squinted and tilted his head. "Some Swede has it I

194

guess." Cliff shook his head slightly. "There's a group message. Tyler was planning on going to the lighthouse. I'm guessing he did."

"Oh. One mystery down."

"Yeah, I'm seeing if he went with anybody, who brought him to the hospital, and that sort of thing. Most of his interactions seem to be through Instagram and Twitter and such. Half these people are in different time zones."

"So, do we go back to the lighthouse?"

"We could. Of course, there is the possibility that you retrace your steps and end up in the body of a 12-year-old boy in 2024."

"It's worth trying, Cliff."

"Just keep Tyler's pants on, we'll figure something out. Did you look at his pictures?"

"I didn't see a camera."

"Oh fer chrissakes. This thing in my hand is a camera, dummy. You're from 2004 not 1904."

"It's a camera phone?"

"Uh, yep. They're all camera phones."

"Fine. So what?"

"The last pictures are from Sunday at the lighthouse."

"Let me see."

"There's videos too." Cliff pulled a white string from his pocket. It forked at one end, and Cliff handed Angela one of those. "Put that in your ear; it's like a headphone." The patronizing tone went unappreciated.

Cliff pushed play and a video began.

"Is that what I look like?" she wondered aloud.

Tyler appeared on the tiny screen. He was at the lighthouse. It looked to be about dusk. He began. "Hello again, and welcome to Agents of the Unknown, the fastest growing paranormal investigation show on all of YouTube."

"What the fuck is YouTube?" asked Angela.

"It's-"

"Shh!"

Cliff made the "but you asked" face. The video continued.

"I stand here in the lighthouse at MacArthur Bay, long thought to be haunted by many a spirit. Two years before the lighthouse opened in 1877, this spot was the site of the horrific crash of the ship, "the Magpie".

"I guess they needed a lighthouse there," Cliff said.

"Shh."

"A dozen souls were lost in the sea that day. The lighthouse became operational in 1879, where it went through an unusually large- we'll cut here."

The video ended. Cliff played with the phone a bit. "Here let's try this one."

"A dozen souls were lost at sea that day. The lighthouse became operational in 1879. Over the decades it experienced a large turnover of staff. The journeys to and from the . . . island. . . were hazardous, and lighthouse operators would go to work, never to be seen again!

"After nearly one hundred years of operation, the lighthouse was deactivated. The land was bought by private investors and used as a crematorium-"

"Columbarium," Cliff corrected.

"Shh."

"Financial problems abounded, tax went unpaid, and the business was shut down in 1986. The lighthouse stands today, as a marker of a bygone era. Of a frob- blewbitty, blah blah- cut."

The video ended. Cliff played with the phone a bit more.

"Who is filming all this? Maybe we can track down him?"

"Looks like selfies."

"What?"

"It looks like Tyler was just holding the phone away from his face. There are cameras in the front and back of the phone. Here, there's more."

A new video started.

"Wish you would've showed up, Joshua. It's gross out here. I got to host this and work the camera. This is bullshit. Yeah, that's right mom; I said bullshit. Deal with it. All right, start actual recording here. . .

"I will be recording audio with this microphone over the course of the next four hours. We will examine the white noise of the waves for EVP."

"That's *electronic* voice phenomenon, it doesn't work with waves, dummy!"

"Shut the fuck up Cliff."

"I have set up my mom's old camcorder to night vision mode to look for any discrepancies that might be caused by wandering spirits. And I, myself, will be staying here all night and keeping a journal of my findings, um, a video journal of my findings. A vlog of my findings, a video log of my findings. . . Yeah, I think video log sounds best. Cut it here."

"See that?" Cliff pointed to the stopped video.

"What? You think you see something?" Angela felt a new sense of hope.

"I think he's holding a selfie stick. He must be zoomed in."

The new hope diminished.

"Where's the rest?" she asked.

"That's it. I mean, unless you have the camcorder."

"Shit. Susan has it."

"Who's Susan?" Cliff asked.

"Tyler's mom," Angela explained.

"Let's go get that camera."

"Let's just go straight to the source and check out the lighthouse. Do you have a

canoe? Wait, did Tyler have a
canoe? How did he get over
there? It didn't look like he
swam. Maybe he-"

   "Hold up. If you want to go
to the lighthouse, I'll take
you to the lighthouse."

   "But . . .?"

   "But first, I have to take
you someplace else. Give me
five minutes to make a phone
call."

   "Really?"

   "Maybe three."

MINUS SEVEN

For her twelfth birthday
Angela wanted to go to
Agostino's pizza with a few
friends. That's what Shannon
had done for her birthday.
Against her sister's wishes,
their mother had brought Angela
along for Shannon's super adult
and not at all little kid-ish
get-together. It was way cooler
than a party. They were hanging
out. They didn't sing stupid
songs or play stupid games or
wear stupid hats. They were
cool.

Sure, Shannon had been
turning fifteen and Angela was
still another year away from
being even the lowliest
teenager. But twelve was still
a big deal, and she was every
bit as mature as Shannon. Her
grades were better, she did
well in track, and her band
teacher said she was "showing

promise" on the clarinet. Shannon couldn't manage her money, but Angela saved up enough, on her own, to buy a Charlotte Hornets Starter hoodie.

Really, Angela ought to have been the older sister. That would have been fair.

Sunday had not gotten off to a great start. Angela thought she would wake up to a big birthday breakfast, but instead woke up to the sounds of somebody throwing up in the bathroom. Maybe Shannon got drunk like when Becky did on that episode of "Roseanne."

Angela opened her bedroom door to find her dad waiting there. His hair was uncombed and he was still wearing his pajama pants and white t-shirt. "Hey there, kiddo. Happy Birthday! Listen, mom's not feeling too good right now."

"Oh, okay."

"I'm just going to leave her be until about eleven or so," dad explained. "We'll still have your party even if mom has to stay home."

"Okay."

"There's a deposit," he said smiling a crazy Gomez Addams smile. Dad pushed some curly hairs off his forehead, but they popped right back as soon as his hand was gone. "Anyway, I'm sorry, but I don't know how to make your birthday waffles."

Dad was afraid of the waffle iron. Last time he used it he had managed to set off the smoke alarm, fall off the ladder while turning off the smoke alarm, and fling the bowl of waffle batter all over the kitchen.

"But I did make some California style French toast and some slightly sweet scrambled eggs that weren't at all made from the leftover egg from the French toast." Dad

205

gave her a slightly apologetic look and Angela smiled weakly.

"Okay." Angela stared at her foot. "I hope mom feels better."

"Me too," Dad agreed. "Listen, we're still going to have fun today. All right?"

"All right."

"As long as you're not expecting a pony, I think today is going to be pretty good. And you'll still get fireworks, no matter what."

"Yeah. Okay. I'll be out in a few minutes, okay?"

"All right, kiddo."

Angela wasn't expecting a pony. She didn't want a big party; she wanted a small adult lunch. She did like the fireworks, though. Having a July 3rd birthday did come with the perk of birthday fireworks. Well, at least half the time it did. She felt uneasy, nervous about the day and nervous about being twelve.

After her non-waffle breakfast, dad let her open some of her presents. They consisted of a shirt mom picked out, a cassette that Angela had asked for last month and one cassette she definitely hadn't asked for ever. Why did her dad think she liked All-4-One? Shannon had probably picked this one out for herself. Where was she anyway?

Angela asked Dad.

"Shannon spent the night at Jessica's. We're gonna pick her up after your party."

Some sister! She couldn't even be bothered to show up to a birthday party? Angela went to her room to pout and listen to her new cassette. She moved her oblong black boom box onto her nightstand, carefully slid the tape in and then slammed herself onto her bed. She plugged in her headphones, which had seen better days. The foam was crumbling apart on the left side, and she could feel the cool metal up against that ear. The headband pulled her hair whenever she took them off. Worst of all, there was a crimp in the wire, so that when she leaned back, no sound came out of the right speaker. Angela thought about ditching the headphones entirely, but Mom was lying down and needed rest. Even if it is your birthday, you can still get in trouble for waking up a sick mom.

Angela turned the tape over, grabbed a magazine, and attempted to read the magazine hanging upside down off her bed. She thought it would look really cool and her dad wouldn't understand it at all.

Before she knew it, it was eleven o'clock. She was supposed to do something at eleven o'clock. Did she have to check on her mom?

She went to her parents' door to do that thing, and heard their voices from the hall.

"Stay in bed, Linda. You still look awful."

She could hear Mom respond, "Thanks a lot."

"Listen, I'm not even going try to spare your feelings here. You look like hammered shit. Stay in bed."

"Tom, it's my little girl's birthday. I just need to take a shower, and I'll be ready to go in thirty minutes."

"What's wrong with your mouth?"

"I think I hurt my jaw throwing up."

"My poor Leen-duh."

"I'll be fine."

Angela heard her father come towards the door, and suddenly

she became terrified. She
hopped back to her room and
quickly put her headphones back
on. They weren't even plugged
in anymore.

Dad came out of his room and
stood at her threshold. "We're
leaving in half an hour."

"Cool. How's mom doing?"

"She's . . . okay."

Mom came out of her bedroom
twenty-five minutes later. She
looked all right to Angela,
though maybe a little tired.
She was wearing her locket, and
the ear-rings that Angela
always thought looked like
starfish. "Happy Birthday!
Sorry, I couldn't make you your
breakfast."

"It's okay mom. You make me
breakfast all the time." Angela
did her best to sound like it
was no big deal. She guessed
that it really wasn't a big
deal. It was her birthday,
after all. Why waste it moping

about French toast and annoying
R&B groups?

"You're a pretty good kid."

"Thanks mom."

"I love you, punkin."

"Okay, okay." Twelve-year-
olds can't stomach this mushy
stuff.

Angela's heart sank as they
drove past Agostino's Pizza.
Then they passed Maxi's Pizza,
and she got nervous. Her
worries were confirmed when
they pulled into the parking
lot of the Pizza Castle. But
maybe it wasn't so bad. You
could still have an adult
birthday party at a Pizza
Castle.

Right?

Her dad led them to the
party room. There were
balloons. There was a tissue
paper table cloth with cartoon

characters on it. She didn't
even watch those cartoons. This
wasn't at all right. Angela
could feel her face getting
warmer.

A few kids from school were
already there, but there was no
sign of her best friend Nicole.
She asked Dad and he leaned in
to tell her that Nicole was in
the Catskills with her family.
Lisa wasn't there either. Dad
said she had RSVPed, but maybe
she was sick like Mom.

Mom looked worse and worse
since the car ride. She was
slumped on a bench next to the
jukebox, nursing one of those
thick plastic glasses of water
with the bumps on the side.
After twenty minutes of being
miserable, Dad told her that he
was going to get Uncle Ron to
drive her home. Mom said no.

There were tense
negotiations.

Finally, Mom said, "I'll
just lay down in the car for

212

ten minutes, then I'll come back in in time for cake and presents." Mom was pale and sweaty.

"It's 85 degrees out outside. You're not going to sit in the car."

"I'll roll down all the windows; I'll be fine." Mom pushed herself to her feet. She wobbled a bit, and Uncle Ron grabbed her under the armpit.

Dad gave in, and with Uncle Ron, helped mom out to the car.

What could Angela do? Her mom was sick, her dad had to tend to her mom, and here she was at a birthday party she didn't want with baby decorations and surrounded by kids she didn't really like. Her own sister couldn't even be bothered to show up.

But what could she do? Angela sat at the table, mortified, but trying not to pout. She was a good girl. She wasn't going to throw a tantrum like a spoiled brat. Angela felt like she was doing a good job keeping all of the disappointment from showing on her face.

Dad got back just before the pizzas arrived. Cheerily, he gave her the very first slice: pepperoni pizza. Angela didn't like pepperoni anymore. She hadn't liked pepperoni for two years and meticulously picked off each piece. She wasn't even sure that she was feeling hungry. Her insides ached.

How did her parents know so little about her? Did anybody here know who she really was?

Mom didn't make it back for the cake. She wasn't missing much. It was one of those grocery store chocolate cakes where the chocolate was way too dark and the frosting just tasted like whipped cream. Happy Birthday was written in this ugly green icing that looked like Nickelodeon slime.

The melted wax from the birthday candles looked more appetizing.

Angela wanted to go home, but she stayed and opened presents bought and brought by the moms of kids she barely knew. She opened a toy she already had, a dress that was two sizes too big, a clock radio (who gets a kid a clock radio?), and a booklet of fifteen one-dollar McDonalds gift certificates. Gift certificates! Adults gave her these books all the time. Did they make their kids buy their own food? Angela's parents were kind enough people to supply both room and board to their children. They never asked her to pick up the check at restaurants.

But with each gift Angela smiled, and made eye contact with the giver, and said thank you. She just wanted to be home. Her dad had one more box in his hand. He passed it to Angela and said, "Last one." He

gave a weak grin; he wanted to
be home too.

Angela examined the box
carefully. It was wrapped in
the Sunday comics, which meant
that Dad had been the one to
wrap it. She poked a finger
into the face of Slylock Fox,
and peeled the paper back.

It was perfect.

She hadn't even asked for
these.

Inside the box were the big,
square headphones she had been
dreaming of ever since she saw
them in the Sears Wishbook last
year.

Angela could feel her eyes
fill up with tears. "Thanks,
Dad. These are just what I
wanted."

"It was all your mom. I just
wrapped it."

"Well, I have to go out and
thank her."

"All right. Just be careful in the parking lot."

Angela ran out of the Pizza Castle, and for a moment forgot where they had parked. She found their escort wagon right under the same shady elm they had parked by two hours ago.

Her mom was lying down in the passenger seat with her eyes open. She had been dead for twenty minutes.

SEVEN

Cliff's car was shockingly clean and comfortable on the inside considering what it looked like on the outside. Its front bumper was held on by duct tape and cable ties, the front left fender was dimpled like a golf ball, the roof was ever so slightly caved in, and Angela was pretty sure that the bumper stickers on the back were load-bearing.

It made her wonder if Gomez were still running somewhere.

"Cliff, where are we going?" Angela asked with growing impatience.

Angela had been in the car with Cliff for more than half an hour, and she was growing restless. She lost all sense of what time it was.

Maybe that was fitting.

"We're almost there." Cliff assured.

"That isn't what I asked." The longer they drove, the quieter Cliff became. Something seemed off. Cliff was never quiet. But maybe that's not true anymore. Maybe 2014 Cliff is a quiet guy.

Do people change that much?

No matter. Angela couldn't take any more quiet tonight. She had had quite enough. "Do you think if I go back in time to the past, that I'll mess up the space-time continuum and send this version of you into oblivion?"

Cliff smiled. "Well, that would suck, but if comics taught me anything, you'd just create another branch in the timeline. That's what happened when Superman tried to save Lincoln." Cliff spoke with a confident authority that Angela could not imagine was merited.

She raised an eyebrow. "I thought you didn't believe in stuff like that anymore?"

"I don't think I do." Cliff sighed. "But if the universe is infinite in time and space, then anything with even one-one billionth of a chance of happening is happening constantly. Well, maybe it is. I dunno, boss."

Angela shrugged. "It certainly seems like a lot of weird things can happen to me."

"It seems to you like a lot of weird things can happen or it seems like a lot of weird things happen to you?"

"Fucking both," Angela answered.

"Can't argue with that. I tell ya, if we figure out how to send you back in time, there are really only three things to do."

"Really?"

"One: kill Hitler. Two: visit dinosaurs. Three: buy stock," Cliff declared.

"I don't plan on going back any further than 2004, Cliff."

"Well, I can still give you some stock tips," he responded.

"I'll buy a sports almanac, too."

Cliff turned down a residential street, and slowed down.

"Well, if you do memorize the Super Bowl winners, give past me a cut of that action."

"All right," Angela accepted. "Hey, Cliff?"

"What?"

"What's the deal with the number sign everywhere?"

Cliff cocked an eyebrow. "How do you mean?"

"I saw it on the phone, the coffee shop menu and a shirt

and a billboard. Pound Selfie.
Pound Coffee. Number Coffee?
Sharp coffee? I'm trying to
remember my clarinet years."

"Oh. Hashtag."

"Huh?"

"The kids use the number
sign as 'hashtag' and it is
used for stuff like tweeting.
Tweeting, that's like micro-
blogging." Cliff stopped for a
minute to figure out the best
way to explain this thing.
"It's like everybody is texting
into the ether, and you can
search through all these text
messages more easily by using
these specific hashtags."

"So, like those old AOL
keywords?"

"Yeah. Well, kinda." The car
slowed even more. "We're here."

Angela made another mental
note to memorize the Super Bowl
winners as Cliff pulled into a
driveway on a quiet side
street. Both got out of the

car, and Angela followed Cliff up the front porch steps of a cozy house, the color of a Spanish olive.

"Where are we?"

"You'll see."

"I know I'll fucking see. Why can't you just tell me?"

They took three stairs up, approaching a dark green door with a diamond shaped window. A dog started barking before Cliff got the chance to knock.

The front porch light came on.

Angela could hear locks being turned on the other side.

A woman appeared from behind the door and said, "Cliff, what bullshit are you driving out here for?"

Angela blurted out a single word. She tried to stop herself because she knew it was the wrong thing to say. But the word hung in between the three of them, and time froze.

"Mom?"

Sure, the woman who opened the door resembled her mom; that is, if her mom had tattoos up and down her arms. Upon a longer glance, Angela spotted more and more differences and knew it wasn't her mother. That would be impossible. Her mom died more than a decade ago. No, wait: more than two decades ago.

No, the woman wasn't her mother, but who she was seemed no less impossible.

She felt a tightening in her gut.

"Angela, do I have a story for you," Cliff proclaimed to the woman at the door.

Once, when Angela was in second grade, she went to school with the flu. Of course, she had a good reason: She didn't want to miss being in the Christmas pageant.

She was the captain of the sheep, after all.

When Ms. Dorothy first announced that they were putting on a play, Angela was very excited. She had wanted desperately to be Mary, which was usually the only girl part in all these Christmas shows. Joseph, Jesus, the wise men, the shepherds, the inn-keepers, God, and the camels, those were all boy parts. Sure, girls could play them, but they weren't girl parts.

The role of Mary went to a fifth grader, though. The fifth graders got all the good parts. Even Shannon who didn't care

about anything got a good part.
It was a boy part but she got
two lines.

There were only ten sixth
graders in the whole school,
and only one of them wanted to
be a wise man. Angela didn't
understand them at all.

The fourth graders were all
shepherds, just like Linus and
Shermy.

The third graders were all
donkeys. Angela was still a
little afraid of donkeys
because of *Pinocchio*.

The second graders, like
her, were all sheep.

The first graders were all
clowns; Angela wasn't quite
sure how their musical number
about clowning around fit with
the narrative of the nativity,
but she was sure that Ms.
Dorothy knew what she was
doing.

The kindergarteners were all
angels; boy, that was a laugh.

Angela had heard that Frank Smith had bitten Jesse Petrowski right in the spine when they were playing with the fifty states puzzle after naptime. Another time Audra Pudlewski pushed Janelle Maiorano off of a stool because she called herself a princess. Those kids were monsters.

Angela figured that if she was stuck being a sheep, she at least got to be captain of the sheep. Ms. Dorothy had put her in charge of all the rest of the sheep, which meant that she had the most important part during the second grade song. She got to boss around the sheep that were jumping in front of baby Jesus in order to help him to fall asleep. Angela enjoyed rhyming sleep with sheep, so she enjoyed singing the song around the house. It also annoyed Shannon and that was a bonus.

Then, the night before the big show, Angela started to feel terrible. At first, she thought that she had eaten too much of Dad's cottage pie, but realized later that she had eaten less than she normally did. Dad made cottage pie once a month. He made dinner once a month and it was always cottage pie. Angela would eat the potatoes off the top, pick a few peas out and eat the barest minimum of the meat.

That night, her skin felt sore, and she was really cold and tired. She took her bath early and went to bed right after. Mom asked if she was feeling all right, and Angela told her that she just wanted to rest up for the show. She wasn't lying. She did want to rest up for the show. But it felt like a lie and that made Angela feel guilty.

In the morning, she felt even worse. It didn't help that her big sister Shannon had woken her up by shaking her and yelling, "Get up, lazybones!" Shannon, being one of those privileged fifth graders, was

cast as one of the innkeepers
that turned away Joseph and
Mary. She was a villain. Angela
thought Shannon was a natural
villain.

Still, though, Shannon was a
villain with *two whole lines*.

Angela went to the bathroom,
brushed her teeth haphazardly,
and brushed her hair somewhat
less thoroughly than could be
described as haphazardly. She
packed her bookbag, went to the
kitchen and ate her runny
oatmeal very slowly. She
watched it slide off the sides
of the spoon. Mom always made
the oatmeal with too much milk;
it always made it look like hot
pudding. Dad, on the other
hand, would use no milk and
just the tiniest bit of water
so that the oatmeal would come
out looking like they were
eating Thanksgiving stuffing
for breakfast.

Angela stared at her cereal
and her mind wandered. *Maybe
I'm like Goldilocks*, she

thought. *Did she eat oatmeal? Or was it porridge? Is porridge like oatmeal?*

"We're leaving in five minutes, Angela."

"All right," Angela replied, knowing that mom had meant *hurry up*.

The car ride made Angela feel worse, so getting out of the car made her feel relatively better. She suffered slightly through attendance, and was barely able to finish her spelling test within the allotted time.

But it really wasn't that bad. She knew she would feel better when the show started. The show must go on! And they can't do a nativity story without a sheep captain. That would be ridiculous.

Before she knew it, she was wearing a paper sheep costume and sitting on a steel folding chair in the auditorium-slash-gymnasium-slash-lunchroom-slash-makeshift church while the chapel was under renovation. Angela was feeling a little sweaty and dizzy, but she knew she would have a lot of time to sit and watch the clowns and the angels and the goings-on of Baby Jesus and the Ovnazareth family.

By the time she had to perform, Angela barely remembered that she was sick. She went up in front of all those parents, Father Archie, and the sisters, determined to be the best sheep captain she could be.

For the first verse, things were going smoothly. Ms. Dorothy was playing the piano, the sheep were jumping, the baby Jesus was starting to sleep, probably.

Things went wrong during the first chorus. Angela felt a tickle in her throat as she was dancing by Mary and Joseph. She just needed to stop dancing for a second. Just for a second and then she'd be fine.

But before she could even realize what was happening, Angela started vomiting.

Into the manger.

Directly onto the baby Jesus.

Thankfully, it was just a Cabbage Patch Kid and not the real baby Jesus. Though, the real baby Jesus probably could've just healed her and stopped her from throwing up altogether.

Half of the sheep stopped singing and dancing right away. Some continued on at half speed, even though Ms. Dorothy wasn't playing the piano anymore. Danielle Evans ran off the stage, crying.

What were they supposed to do without their captain? Of course, they would falter. The captain goes down with his sheep.

The next thing Angela knew, she was in the car. Dad was driving them home, and Mom was sitting in the back seat next to her. Angela was half-asleep, her head on her mother's lap. She occasionally glanced up to see the light shining off of her mother's locket. Mom told her, "Try to get some rest, okay, punkin." Mom didn't seem at all mad at her for her for puking on the baby Jesus. That must be one of the biggest sins you could do, right?

Mom wasn't mad. She stroked Angela's hair, sweeping sweaty bangs off of her forehead. She quietly sang a song as Angela fell back asleep, a song about swimming the seas to ease her pain. It was the same song she always sang to Angela.

Angela spent the next day on the couch, with the ugly beige mop bucket near her on the floor. Her mom made her soup and brought her 7-up. They watched "The Price is Right" together, then two episodes of

233

"Mr. Ed". Ten minutes into the "Donna Reed Show", Angela was sleeping, her head on her mother's lap for a second time in as many days.

EIGHT

"You've misled this kid if you told him I'm his mom," the woman Angela said. "I'd remember a thing like that."

"I," said the boy Angela before stopping abruptly. She didn't know what else she wanted to say. Running away seemed to be a good option.

She did that thing.

She didn't know where she was. She didn't know where she was going. She didn't even really know why she was running. She felt like burrowing underground, but running was a decent second choice.

Maybe it was a stupid thing to do.

Maybe her future self, her present self, remembered how to get back to the present, the past.

But that version of her didn't recognize the Tyler version of herself on the porch. She didn't remember this meeting.

Maybe I don't make it back.

But, no, Angela thought. *I must make it back. There I am!*

Maybe I'm not supposed to be here. Maybe it's a mistake. Maybe I'm a mistake. Maybe that's not me. Maybe I'm not me.

I don't like this.

I don't like this at all.

So, she ran.

And she kept on running.

Why wouldn't I remember being Tyler?

Tyler's body was adept at running. Angela was never so good at it. She found a rhythm. Each step felt easier than the last.

Maybe that was Tyler and Tyler has been me for the last ten years. But no, he would have recognized himself.

Right?

She took in air through her Tyler's nose, and breathed out through his mouth.

She focused on the rhythm of running. Every time her mind started to whir, she stopped it before it could gain momentum.

She kept on running.

Forty minutes had passed before she slowed down.

Ten more minutes passed before she stopped.

She didn't have any answers to her questions.

She didn't know where she was, aside from the parking lot of some restaurant. She could see the glow of the neon sign in her peripheral vision.

Angela looked up at it: it was a Pizza Castle. She loosely covered her mouth and nose with her left hand and began to chuckle. "Fuck you, too, God." She sat on the curb, near a big green mailbox, the kind that was only for use by mailmen.

She sat there and thought about this mailbox that she would never be able to use. Everything else seemed too big.

But she could think about this mailbox. It looked just like the blue ones, but didn't have a little sideways door on top. On the blue ones, you could pull the handle of the little door and make a tray for your envelopes, and then when you let go, the tray would become a slide.

A beaten-up Honda Accord narrowly avoided a rear end collision as it slowed suddenly and pulled into the parking lot in front of Angela. The car turned around in the lot so that its passenger side was right up against her.

The window came down.

From behind it, a teenaged girl yelled, "Tyler, what the hell is wrong with you?" She had curly hair, a pointed nose and wore a lot of eyeliner.

"I'm. . . sorry?"

"What are you doing here? Get in the car!"

Angela grabbed the handle to the back door, and weighed her options.

"Your mom is worried sick." The girl continued. "You won't answer my texts. You didn't even tell me you were at the hospital."

"Should I shut the car off?" the driver asked.

"No. He's getting in."

Angela took a guess, "Hannah?" Then she opened the door.

Angela rode in the back of the Honda. Hannah had moved back there, as well, walking around the front of the car and getting in behind the driver before they left the parking lot. The driver, some athletic kid with dark features who was maybe twenty, stayed mostly quiet up front, occasionally glancing in the rear-view mirror.

"You're out here, god knows where, with no money, no ID, standing in a parking lot. You're dripping with sweat. Are you on drugs?"

"I was sitting. I was running." Angela replied, prompting an angry look from Hannah.

"In the middle of the night in the middle of nowhere?

Tyler, you have to take care of yourself."

"Where are we going?" Angela asked.

"I'm taking you home," Hannah answered.

"Can we not? Can we not go there?" She took off her glasses and wiped the sweat off her face with her sleeve.

"You got some place else you need to be?" asked the driver.

Angela looked down. She didn't know how to answer.

"Tyler, I worry about you." The stranger stared at Angela, pleading and compassionate. "You know?"

Angela laughed quietly and pinched the bridge of her nose with her left hand. "No," she said.

"Well I do." Most of the compassion was gone. "I'm sorry to have to track you down like this, but you really left me no choice."

"How did you find me?" Angela wondered out loud.

"How would I not find you? I know all your passwords, Tyler. I can track your phone. You're on my find a friend app. I literally always know where you are."

"You can do all that?" Angela pondered. "Like triangulate the coordinates?"

"Anybody can do that." The rest of the compassion had left Hannah's voice. "What is wrong with you? Seriously."

Angela slouched in her seat. "You wouldn't believe me if I told you. It's weird."

Hannah giggled. "Tyler, honey, when we were eleven you told me that you could control the weather if I gave you a day's notice. You promised me a snow day, and I believed you. I got a C on a spelling test because of you."

"She still pissed about that C, man. I told ya!" The driver added.

Annoyed, Hannah continued, "Just last month, you kept me on the phone for an hour talking about how a zombie virus could be spread through New York City via bedbugs. You've told me, several times in fact, that Mr. Krzal was a stretched-out little person!"

"Like a midget?" Angela asked the frustrated Hannah.

"That one is true," the driver chimed in. "He had that surgery where they break your arms and legs and reset them to make you tall! Well, taller."

Hannah sighed. "The point is: I listen to your crazy stories. I've spent half my life listening to your crazy stories. You're acting like this is something new." She stopped and turned her attention to the driver. "Josh, how long until we get to Tyler's house?"

"Half hour or so," responded the driver.

"See, the boyfriend says you got half an hour to tell me your crazy story."

"Boyfriend? Yours or mine?" Angela was half-interested in the geometry of these relationships.

"Mine, ya dummy, though sometimes I wonder."

"She totally ships us!" Josh interjected.

The concern on Hannah's face grew. "How messed up is your head?"

"Fine." Angela smiled. "My name is Angela Brooks. I was born in Pittsburgh Pennsylvania on July third in 1981."

"Be serious."

"Shit, dude," said Josh. "Was the lighthouse actually haunted? Are you possessed?"

"No," Angela replied. Then she paused to think about the question for a bit. "Well, not by a ghost. I don't know what's going on. I blacked out in 2004 as Angela, and woke up Monday night in 2014 as Tyler."

"Tyler, remember when we were kids and you said that the car headlights hurt you because you thought you were part vampire?" Hannah condescended. "You get these things in your head and-"

"No. I don't," Angela corrected. "I don't know anything about Tyler. I know next to nothing about the last ten years of everything. I just want to go home. To my home, though, not to Tyler's."

Josh spoke up again. "Maybe when you blacked out in 2004, you had a heart attack and died or something. Now you're like a ghost, and you've possessed Tyler and we have to exorcise you so that you can step into the light and leave our friend alone."

"I'm not dead!" Angela demanded.

"Dead people don't even know that they are dead half the time. Like in *the Sixth Sense*," Josh asserted. "Did that come out when you were still alive? That's kinda old, right?"

"Yes, I know that movie and no, it's not like that. Somebody just took me to see 2014 Angela, and she wasn't a dead person. She was just there, and she was me but not."

"You met future you? Aw, that's fucking trippy. Did you guys-"

"Stop it!" Hannah demanded.

"Hold on," Josh implored. "What did you say to *you*? And what did *you* say to you?"

"I ran away," Angela responded.

"Why'd you do that?"

"Seemed like a good idea at the time."

"Be straight with me," Hannah demanded.

"Look, I'm really scared. I've been scared. I don't know."

Hannah unbuckled her seatbelt and slid closer to Angela. She hugged her. "It's going to be all right."

Angela went to pull away from the hug, but gave in to it.

"It's going to be all right," Hannah repeated.

"How do you know?"

Hannah started to say something but Josh interrupted, "Because we are gonna go back to that lighthouse, right now."

"Okay. Sit down and I'll tell you. When I was about your age, your grandpa, not Grandpa Jack but your other grandpa who died before you were born, my dad, well, his name was Eugene.

"He worked a lot of different jobs, and we moved around a bit and he was gone a lot. Sometimes it was for his job and sometimes it was to look for a better job. He wanted to be able to make sure we could live a good life, you know?

"Now, your Aunt Alice, she was always kinda happy to see our dad go. He wouldn't let the family watch TV when we ate dinner. Grandma, she didn't care as long as we cleaned our plates. Plus, I think she rather be watching "My Three Sons," too.

"But, anyway, every time our dad would go, I would cry. And he hated that. It wasn't that he was annoyed, but he probably was. I think it broke his heart." She smiled a sad, proud smile.

"My dad, he always wore slip on shoes, loafers. He had this maroon pair that looked like a really fancy car to me. I could picture tail fins and chrome on them, just like those big, old Chevys. They had little diamond shaped indents towards the top; the shoes, not the Chevys. And somehow it became fashionable to put a penny in there.

"So, one day, to stop me from crying, he gets down on one knee and takes the penny out of his loafer. He says to me, 'don't cry, angel face.' And he hands me the penny. He says, 'you know I'm going to come back soon; you've got my best penny.'

"And every time he left after that, he bent down on one knee and took out his penny."

"And he always came back?" Angela asked.

"And he always came back," Linda lied. She smiled and closed the locket. "Now go to sleep, okay, punkin?"

NINE

The first thing Angela noticed was the sign which read "No Trespassing - Private Property." The second was, "A bridge? They built a fucking bridge?"

"Yeah," Josh replied and then asked, "Hasn't that always been there?"

"No. I had to take a goddamned canoe out there!" Angela studied the long rope bridge and its battered wooden steps. "Son of a bitch."

"It's weird hearing you swear so much," Josh noted.

"They're not even using- why is it weird? Is profanity outlawed here in the future, like in *Demolition Man*?"

"*Demolition Man*?" asked Hannah.

Josh smiled. "Ignore her; she doesn't know what the three seashells are for. Naw, it's weird because Tyler's family is like super-Christian or something."

"Super-Christian is my least favorite person on the Justice League." Angela looked at the lighthouse and wanted a cigarette.

"I don't know if I've said this yet, but if you two are just playing a joke on me, you guys are dead." Hannah stared at Josh, waiting for him to crack.

"Baby, I'm not in on this. The joke would be on me too."

Hannah scrunched up her nose.

"I am an innocent man," Josh proclaimed.

"This is no time to quote Billy Joel," Angela declared.

"Who?" came Josh's response.

"Never mind."

"Listen, I've made a bunch of videos with Tyler. You can believe me: He's not that good of an actor. So, I think he's either telling the truth or completely nuts."

"I guess." Hannah agreed.

Angela rolled her eyes.

"This is a level of commitment to a part that Tyler just doesn't have. He's walking differently, he sounds different. Let me show you," Josh said to Hannah before turning to Angela. "Angela, can you walk away from us, back toward us and then tell us a joke?"

"What? No." Since Josh was trying to help, she didn't tell him to fuck off.

"See," Josh said. "Tyler would have done it and told the hamster joke."

"OK. You win. Is the bridge safe?" asked Hannah.

"Oh yeah, I've been on it a bunch of times," reassured Josh. Nevertheless, he tested the first step carefully before putting his weight on it. "See. It's fine. C'mon."

Angela followed Josh. Hannah followed Angela. The bridge was sturdier than it looked, but that fact provided little comfort to the three.

Josh carefully checked each of his steps, Hannah tried to hurry the group forward to get off as quickly as possible, and Angela was squished in the middle. After what felt like a long time to Angela, all three stepped off the bridge and onto the crag.

"Now what?"

"I don't know," Josh stated. "I didn't really think that far ahead."

"Yeah, me neither," Angela agreed. "I was kinda hoping that something would just happen."

"Well, we can always just take you back to Tyler's mom," suggested Hannah.

Angela ignored the suggestion. "I'm going to poke around inside the lighthouse."

She did that thing.

Hannah and Josh waited outside and stared at their phones. Five minutes later, Angela emerged.

"Well?" Hannah asked, slipping her phone into her back pocket.

"I don't know. No sign of me, no sign of 2004, no sign of Tyler. I wish I knew what I was supposed to be doing."

"Well, I'll double check with you." Josh went inside the lighthouse and examined the stones carefully with his phone's flashlight. Angela stood behind him, trying to remember what everything looked like and what might have changed. She didn't see the 1911 brick or the hole they had made in 2004, just newer stones in the places they used to be.

"Anything?" he asked.

"Same shit," she answered.

Angela punched the newer stones, scraping the skin off of Tyler's knuckles. "Your friend is soft."

They walked back to Hannah.

"Nothing?" she asked.

"Nothing." Angela answered.

"Now what?"

"Let's just sit, and think about things a bit," Josh suggested. "I'm going to go get some blankets from my car. We can sit for a bit and sort things out. I might have some band-aids in my glove box, too."

"Band-aids?" Angela asked. She looked down at her fist, and noticed it was dripping blood. "Oh."

"I'll be right back."

"Listen, I hope you guys don't take my annoyance about this situation personally. I'm trying not to be a bitch here, and, uh. . ." Angela placed her bleeding fist into the pocket of Tyler's hoodie, and applied pressure on both fist and hoodie with the other hand. "Well, thank you, you guys. Thanks for taking me here and being here with me. I appreciate it."

"Hey, it's not your fault," Hannah proclaimed.

"We'd do anything for Tyler," Josh said as he approached the bridge.

"Josh!"

"What? It's true." He stopped moving and turned his attention to Hannah and Angela. "Listen, if you're Angela and we help you get back to whatever, we are helping Tyler. If you're Tyler and you've gone bug nutty, then we are still helping Tyler. If, and now hear me out, you are a demon possessing Tyler and-"

"I'm not a goddamned demon," Angela barked.

"Fine. But before I leave you here alone with my girlfriend, I'd like you to touch my crucifix."

"You were going to just leave a second ago."

"Yeah, but I just thought of this," Josh admitted

"For serious?" she asked

"For serious," he answered.

Angela grunted and raised an eyebrow, but ultimately walked

over to Josh and did as he asked. She wanted a blanket.

Josh looked into Angela's eyes as they both held the crucifix. "All right," he said, "now tell the hamster joke."

"Shut up."

"Okeydokey, I'll be right back with the blankets." He left.

Angela leaned up against the lighthouse and once again wished she had a cigarette. Her body didn't crave the nicotine, but she felt like she needed the routine. Hannah sat on a rock and played with her phone.

"You get a cell signal here?" Angela asked.

"Yeah. I've got a signal everywhere."

"You ever been to Montana?"

"What?"

"Never mind. What are you doing on your phone?" Angela asked.

"I'm texting our moms to let them know where we are."

"What?" For a moment Angela could picture Ms. Clark storming the waterfront with a score of police cars.

"Oh, no, not your mom. I mean, Tyler's mom. Like I texted my mom and Josh's mom, not Mrs. Clark. I'm not that dumb."

"Oh." Angela checked on her fist. The bleeding stopped, but now the knuckle was sticking to the cotton of the sweater pocket.

"Sorry. I'm almost done," Hanna said. "It's rude to be on my phone. Though, I will admit it is easier than trying to figure this situation out."

"That's fair." This hoodie was definitely going to need a wash.

Hannah put the phone back into her pants pocket. "See, all done."

"So, you, Josh and Tyler: what's going on with this 'Three's Company' relationship you guys got?"

"Three is company?"

"Yeah, well, I guess that's not really apt. I mean that's two girls to one guy."

"Uh-huh," Hannah replied, a bit confused.

"Archie, Betty and Veronica are the same thing. It's usually two girls to one guy."

"I don't know who those people are."

"Really?"

"Is it like team Edward and Team Jacob? That's a girl with two guys."

Angela smiled and shook her head. "I don't know who those people are."

"Edward Cullen, sparkly vampire?"

"I know those words, but that doesn't make any sense."

"Really? *Twilight* is everything." Hannah smiled wildly and then let the smile dwindle. "I mean, it's dumb, but, you know?" They listened to the waves. Angela stared out onto the shore; the Pizza Castle that used to be there was now a credit union.

"What I was asking, without the filter of apparently dated and irrelevant pop-culture is: what is this relationship? Josh and you are a couple and Tyler, me, I guess, is a constant third wheel?"

"Well," Hannah thought out loud, "we've all kind of known each other for forever. Josh and I just started dating, really, like a year ago."

"Oh."

"So, maybe you, or Tyler, is like Harry Potter and the two of us are like Ron and Hermione."

"Wait, Ron and Hermione get together?" Angela thought about the wizard and witch, and figured that coupling made sense.

"Spoilers, I guess." Hannah chuckled.

"So, how does Tyler feel about your relationship?"

"IDK." Hannah thought about it for a moment. "He's fine, I guess?"

"No jealousy?"

"Not sexually. He identifies as ace."

"Ace?"

"Asexual."

"What?" Angela was the proper definition of non-plussed. "Is that even a thing?"

"Yeah," Hannah replied, sounding defensive.

"Really? A red-blooded American teenage boy?"

"Yeah." More defensive.

"Does he plan on reproducing by budding?"

"No. He's just, well, sex doesn't matter to him."

"A teenage boy?"

"Why are you hung up on this?"

"It seems hella-sketch," Angela said trying to contain her incredulousness.

"I don't know what to tell you." Hannah turned away.

Yep. A cigarette. Angela really wanted a cigarette.

"I'm not trying to be all judgy. I'm not out to offend you. You gotta understand that I was in a two guy/one girl friend group thing and was wondering how this one worked. You know, it took a while for the dynamic to click."

"Different people are, like, different."

"Yeah, I understand that. There was an unspoken sexual sub-text to my group. You know? I hung out with this guy Robert because I thought he was cute. Robert liked a guy named Cliff because he likes chubby hairy guys. Cliff wanted to fuck me because I was a girl that would talk to him about stuff he cared about like Canadian sketch comedy or Odo. It was a weird little incestuous fire triangle. But the thing is, in my experience at least," Angela paused. She didn't know why she was opening up to this girl. Maybe it felt nice to talk about normal human things for the first time in a long time.

266

She continued, "Well, it's hard to sexualize somebody once you get to know them. It's like the opposite of TV, where eventually everybody has fucked everybody else. I get to know these people as family, and it's just kind of embarrassing to think about them as sexual creatures." Angela felt the cool wind blow on her knuckles, damp with blood. "Maybe that's just because I was raised Catholic."

Hannah didn't have a response. Angela slumped towards the ground. She picked at pebbles on the ground and tried to loosen smaller stones stuck between larger ones.

After a long silence Hannah said, "Tyler is a good person."

"Oh yeah?"

"You'd like him. I mean, I don't know much about you, like, personally. But I think everybody likes Tyler."

"His mom seems about as much fun as a . . . wet blanket." Angela tried to remember one of Cliff's colorful similes, but blanked.

"She's okay. She sold my parent's old house. I mean, she's a little nutty. She *just* let him get an Instagram. She never let him play any video games, at least not anything she thought was violent." Hannah stared off onto the shore. "Tyler's dad's pretty fun."

"I haven't met him. Is he still around?"

Hannah contemplated this for a bit. "Oh, he's away on work right now."

"So, he's like a long-haul trucker or a traveling salesman or something?"

Hannah scrunched up her face. "Traveling salesman? I thought you said you were from

2004? It wasn't that long ago was it? Did they have those?"

Angela gave a hard stare to Hannah, the likes of which she had never seen from Tyler.

"Sorry. No, um, he's an actor. He was just doing community theater stuff on the weekends, mostly. I went to one of his workshops once, whatever you call it with the 'yes, and' stuff. No, but anyway, then he got laid off from his desk job. Tyler's uncle or somebody hooked him up with some sort of cruise ship thing. Uh, gig I guess? He's on the boat for like six months."

"Jesus. He must really want to get away from his wife."

Josh re-appeared carrying blankets. He said, "I've got the blankets," and handed one to Hannah and one to Angela. "Now what?"

"I was just telling Angela about Tyler," Hannah said.

"Oh. That's kinda weird," he replied. "It's like we're talking about Tyler behind his back to his face."

Angela laughed and held her face in her hands. After nearly a minute she stopped laughing and froze in that position.

Josh touched her on the shoulder. "Tyler, Angela, whoever you are, are you all right?"

"Josh, when did you get here?" came the reply.

MINUS TEN

Linda Brooks sat in her
chair, not realizing how long
this day had been until she put
her feet up on the ottoman. She
felt as though she were made
out of jelly. Certainly, the
only things holding her body in
its current shape were her
black jeans and Willie Nelson
T-shirt. Linda sank deeper into
her chair and thought that it
would take a herculean effort
to get her out of this
position.

Why did she agree to have
this Halloween party tomorrow?
She went over the details in
her head and couldn't
understand how she let her
seven-year-old daughter talk
her into throwing a Halloween
party. She should have said,
"Yes, but that means no trick-
or-treating." That could have
been the end of it. Somehow,
Shannon had the guile to get a
party, go trick-or-treating,

and still managed to convince Linda to put together a *Back to the Future* style 50s outfit for her.

Angela, as usual, was easier. For Halloween she just wanted to be Penny from "Inspector Gadget". Even though she was all of four years old, she found everything she needed in the house: an old purse, one of Shannon's old striped shirts, and a green pair of pajama pants that Angela had proclaimed as "perfect" for the costume.

Cheap date, that one.

The girls were quiet now, which was nice if not a bit suspicious. All of Tom's family had told her how lucky she was to have had two girls, and of all of the terrors of having two boys in their house growing up.

Two boys, like that was a lot.

Her best friend growing up was one of twelve kids, eight of whom were boys. Mr. and Mrs. Donnelly just let those kids do whatever the hell they wanted as they had plenty to spare. Linda opened a can of Lone Star beer and thought about calling Mary Donnelly this weekend.

Linda drank a few sips of her beer, then searched for and found the remote to the cable box. She changed the channel to CBS. "The Great Pumpkin" was on tonight and there was going to be some sort of Halloween special starring Garfield. Both of the girls liked Garfield when last she checked; it was hard to keep track of those things with Shannon. If nothing else, it gave them a chance to watch cartoons during the week that weren't those weird-o Nickelodeon things like "Bananaman."

Maybe it was too quiet.

Screw it, Shannon was big enough now to make sure that

Angela didn't stick her finger in a light socket or try to swing from the ceiling fan or otherwise kill herself in all those ways that seem fun to a little kid.

She always kind of imagined that being a parent was a bit like being a prison guard, but she didn't figure that it was like being a prison guard trying to keep all the inmates from hanging themselves with their bedsheets.

They were probably fine.

Still it was awfully quiet.

Soon enough, it wasn't.

From the bedroom came a loud crash followed by a few seconds of silence. Then, screaming.

Every time I open a dang beer. Ah well, mom mode. Linda propelled herself to her feet and rushed down the hall to see Shannon standing in front of Angela.

Shannon had an explanation, as usual. "I was just standing here and she-"

Linda gently moved Shannon off to the side. Maybe it wasn't so bad.

She saw red all over the brown carpet and for just a moment wondered what it was.

Blood was pouring out of Angela's forehead. *Goddamnit.* Linda commanded Shannon, "Get me the red rag from the linen closet and run it under some cold water first."

"But I didn't-"

"Go, get the rag, and run it under cold water."

"Let me look at you, punkin." Angela obeyed as best she could. Her face was one shade of red from crying and another shade of red from bleeding. "It's okay," Linda said, hoping it were true.

Shannon returned with the rag. Linda carefully dabbed at the gash and pulled Angela's hair back. The cut wasn't very deep, but it was long.

Shit.

"Hold this here, punkin," she said to Angela. "Stay with your sister," she said to Shannon. "I'm going to call an ambulance. I'll be right back."

Linda sent Shannon over to the neighbor's house, and rode in the ambulance with Angela. Linda couldn't remember anything about the ambulance ride as soon as she stepped out. The bleeding had stopped, or at least slowed, and there was a bandage on her daughter's head. She didn't remember any of that happening, though. She looked down to her shirt to see that old Willie's head was covered in blood. Dazed, Linda signed in to the emergency room, and was instructed to take a seat and wait.

She did that thing, holding her daughter on her lap and hugging her. Without even realizing it, Linda had started humming the song "If I Needed You."

"Crazy huh?" said a woman with permed brown hair across from her. She was seated on a row of orange plastic chairs and staring at the television that rested on a swivel by the ceiling in the corner.

"What?"

"You didn't hear? Some crazy lady in Philly shot up a mall. Like ten people!"

"I guess I've been out." Linda scrunched up her face. "She killed ten people?"

"Naw. She only killed like two or three," the woman stopped and corrected herself, "That's not to say only two or three, it is still a tragedy and all. It's terrible. I mean, what is with people these days?"

"Something in the water, I reckon." Linda's mother would always say that phrase. Linda found herself saying more of her mother's phrases the older she got.

"Fuck," muttered the woman, more to herself than to Linda. Then she turned her head to the pair and blushed. "Oh, I'm sorry. You got a kid. But you know, I just moved to Pennsylvania, and a thing like this happens. How close is Philly, anyway?"

"Not very," Linda assured her. "It's like five or six hours."

"Crazy world."

"They ought to sell tickets." That was another one of mom's phrases. Boy do these things sneak up on a person. Still distracted by the onset

278

of matronage, Linda asked,
"They get her?"

"Oh yeah. Some ambulance
driver disarmed her and gave
her to mall security. Can you
imagine? Can you imagine that?
A mass murderer being turned
over to the guy that hassles
teens for hanging out in the JC
Penny's?"

"Crazy world."

"Crazy world."

"Did you ever wonder what it
all means?" Linda's face showed
her regret almost immediately.
Asking this to a stranger was a
move which Linda considered to
be about as sane as hitting on
twenty.

Asking a question like that
is how cults get you.

"Life?" The woman didn't
even need to think about the
answer; maybe she was in a
cult. "My crazy old auntie used
to tell me that in the long
term, the only thing worth a

damn is having a bunch of people who need you and depend on you."

"Is that right? But what about the short term?"

"Getting your rocks off." It was now the stranger's turn to demonstrate a look of instant regret.

Linda's eyes widened.

"Auntie's words, not mine. Shit, sorry about the kid, again."

"Welp, she's the result of some of that I reckon."

The stranger smiled. "Aren't we all?"

A nurse called out, "Angela Brooks."

"I got her!" Linda turned to the permed lady. "Hey, be safe out there."

"You too."

TEN

Angela woke up from a deep
sleep. It was that great and
complete sleep that she only
really ever experienced as a
little kid. She felt peaceful
and relaxed for the first time
in what felt like a long time.

Then, she remembered recent
events and every muscle in her
body tensed. She held her eyes
closed, tightly, and took three
deep breaths. Did they sound
like her breaths? Did they
sound like Tyler's breaths?

Who even knew anymore?

Slowly, tentatively, she
opened her eyes. That's when
she was it.

Bigfoot.

She saw bigfoot, or rather
Tyler's poster of bigfoot.

"Mother goddamned fucker!"

She felt like crying, so she did.

Susan knocked on Tyler's bedroom door. "Tyler, honey, is everything okay?"

"Go away," Angela moaned.

"What's the matter?" Susan asked while opening the bedroom door a crack.

"I'm still here. I'm still Tyler."

"Oh, for Pete's sake. I thought you were done with all this nonsense! What's so wrong with being Tyler anyway?" Susan stared at the body of her son, full of conflicting emotions. "I'm leaving in five minutes. I've got to get ready."

Susan left the room, closing the door.

Angela got dressed, feeling a sense of defiance. She was going to win. She rummaged through Tyler's drawers and found his wallet. She grabbed his phone from the desk and left the room. Susan was still there, waiting in the hall.

"Your father and I love you very much, Tyler."

"Tyler's not here, Ms. Clark. I'm gonna go find him." She checked her pockets for all the necessities, wishing that cigarettes were on that list.

"We need Tyler around," Susan announced.

"Yeah, I'm going to try to get him back."

"How would Angela's mom feel if Angela disappeared?"

Part of Angela wanted to grab Susan by the neck, slam her into the wall, and scream obscenities into her face. Instead, she said nothing and left the house.

When she got to the street, she called Cliff. Who else could she call at this point?

He answered on the first ring. "I said I'd email you if I-"

"Cliff, it's Angela."

"Yeah." He said, unimpressed.

"I blacked out for a bit last night. I'm still Tyler. I don't know how I got back to Tyler's house."

"Jeezus," Cliff said, finally reacting to the situation. "You want me to getcha?"

"Please. I don't want to be near his house. Can you get me at the coffee shop?"

"Sure. You gonna run away this time?"

"Look, I'm sorry I ran away. Tyler's friends found me," Angela explained. "I told them the whole, weird situation."

"I know."

"Listen! I went to the lighthouse last night with them. I was trying to force myself back. I don't know what happened. I lost more time. I think Tyler might have come back."

"Darlin', I'll be there as fast as I can. Sit tight, then we'll talk."

Angela made it to the coffee shop and waited outside in the parking lot. It was a surprisingly warm day. Cliff was there twenty-five minutes later.

He pulled sideways across three empty spaces next to Angela. She climbed into Cliff's car, which somehow managed to have a few new dents in it.

"Where should we go?" she asked.

"I thought maybe you'd have an idea about that," was his reply. "Lighthouse?"

"Every time I go there, I go away somewhere and I wake up in a strange bed as Tyler. You know, I don't want to come back as Tyler again, but I think the alternative is not coming back."

Cliff shifted uncomfortably in his chair.

"Cliff, why am I still here? You know, for a minute at the lighthouse last night-"

"Well, now-"

"-I thought that I had to help Tyler out in his life."

"You mean like 'Quantum Leap' Sam Beckett style?" he clarified.

"Yeah, to put right what once went wrong or some bullshit like that. But I don't know. I don't know what would be best for Tyler. I don't even know what would be best for me. I don't know why I am here. And why am I still here? I mean, why is that Angela still here?

287

Future Angela or present Angela or whatever you call her, how is she here when I'm here?"

"Well, darlin', that Angela never left." Cliff pulled the car over. They were on a quiet street with a big shoulder. Angela looked around, but only saw trees and road.

"Where did you take me now?"

"Nowhere."

"You're not going to kill me or anything, right?"

"Naw, I wouldn't do that. It's just, well, I got two things to tell ya. I think I might have learned something new about what's going on. It seems like the sort of thing that requires pulling over. I don't know if you'll like them."

"I didn't even realize that liking it was an option at this point," Angela said, feeling a growing tightness in her chest. "Just tell me."

"I'm still kinda unpacking things here. I'm a little cloudy this morning and am not as sharp as I'd like to be. All right, so, I talked back and forth to Angela for quite a bit. Not you, of course, but present-day Angela. She doesn't remember anything too crazy about that night in the lighthouse. She ripped a hole in the wall, touched some sort of gross gooey stuff. She and Robert poked around a bit, found a used condom and some green pennies, and left."

Angela waited for more to the story, but Cliff stopped there. "That's it? I mean, what's-"

"Naw, so, after they decided to go, Robert accidentally flipped the canoe over while getting back in and they all got soaked. Angela drove home soaking wet sitting on one of those crappy grey car blankets. She was telling me-"

"It's weird hearing me refer to as she. I mean, I'm right here."

"I dig that, but A) this wasn't stuff you experienced and B) I don't want to sound like a *Choose Your Own Adventure* story. Anyways, that's basically the last time Angela thought about the lighthouse. You know, that is until we showed up at her door."

"Really? That's . . . unsatisfying."

"Right. So, I figure there's got to be more to the story. So, we sit around for a bit. We have a beer or three. And I'm just asking about every weird thing that's ever happened to her, to you, to y'all. So, she's talking about throwing up on Jesus, her awful first kiss, that time a runaway girl came to her dad's house claiming to be kidnapped-"

"They didn't wake me up! I slept through the whole thing!"

"And so on. Eventually though, she remembers this weird bit of déjà vu."

"All right," Angela waited.

"So, a few years back, she gets a dog. She and her fiancé are going over names for this dog, cute little Boston-"

"I'm married?"

"Didn't work out. Spoiler alert. Anyways, Angela keeps coming back to this one name: Ilona. Her husband asks where she got the name from, and Angela doesn't really remember. She thinks about it a little more and keeps on coming back to Ilona. She says it out loud a few times and comes up with the name Ilona Hagymasi.

"Angela starts to remember that she had dreams where she was with this woman named Ilona Hagymasi. She remembers what she looks like, she remembers her voice, she remembers what she smelled like, and she remembers dancing with her."

"Okay," Angela replied, wondering where Cliff was going with this story.

"So, Angela looks up her name, and finds an obit. A woman named Ilona Hagymasi died a few years back. Now, everything about this obit seems familiar. Well, no, everything in the first half of the obit seems really familiar, but the second half seems alien. It's like Angela met this woman and was really close friends with her and then they lost touch.

"Except they lost touch in 1980."

"And that was before I was born."

"Uh-huh."

"Maybe my mom knew her?"

"Ilona Hagymasi mean anything to you?"

"No, I've never had any dreams about Ilonas to the very best of my knowledge."

"Then I don't think it's that. And it's not a name like Kevin Smith or Jon Stewart that forty-five people are gonna have in any dang town."

Angela unbuckled her belt and pulled the lever on the side of the seat while leaning back. "When did the dreams about Ilona start?"

"After the lighthouse."

"Oh," she said staring at the dome light. "That's why that Angela has those memories and I don't." She scratched her nose with her left hand.

"I go about some googling."

"Oh fuck." Angela pulled the handle next to her car seat and sat upright. "I'm so dumb." She held her face in her left hand.

"So, the lighthouse-"

Angela's heart was racing. "There's something in the lighthouse that, I dunno, eats memories? Copies memories?"

"So, Angela was hit by, hold up." Cliff regathered his thoughts, "So, Ilona's husband or boyfriend or beau visits the lighthouse and leaves some memories behind. Then Angela is hit by them or something in the lighthouse transfers those memories to her, maybe?"

"Fuck. And Angela got those memories. And Angela leaves a copy of all hers behind."

"That's what we were thinking." Cliff paused. "And you know, if that's the case-"

"I'm not Angela. Fuck." She shook her head. "I can't go back home. Oh, I'm fucked. I'm so fucked. Aw, Jesus." Angela was filled with panic. She couldn't breathe. It felt like her skin hurt. It wasn't really

her and it wasn't really her
skin but it hurt.

Or maybe it was her skin,
her breath, her panic. Was this
her body? Was she really Tyler?

"Well, present tense you
pieced that together faster
than me, too, So I guess I
shouldn't be surprised. I mean,
I was puzzling over that for
months."

Angela took a break from her
panic attack to ask, "What do
you mean *months*?"

"That's the other thing I
had to tell you. Today is
Sunday, July 3rd, 2016. Happy
goddamned birthday, huh?"

Linda was swollen and Linda was hot and Linda was miserable. She was sick of this ugly green couch and this ugly brown carpeting. She had mixed feelings about the sleeping three-year-old on top of her. She felt as though she were having feeling about everything right about now. At that moment, those feelings were as follows:

1. I wish I could move.
2. Shannon has the face of an angel when she is sleeping.
3. I am so glad she is quiet for a change.
4. This kid feels like a dang electric blanket.
5. I wish I could scratch my ankle without waking her.
6. Ugh, that ankle looks huge.
7. I don't want to wake her.

8. Goddamn is my ankle itchy.
9. Thinking about it makes it worse.
10. What time is it?
11. I have seen this commercial for Martini & Rossi Asti Spumante six times already.
12. It's only supposed to get up to 73 today. It feels hotter.
13. I can't see the clock.
14. I sure can hear it though.
15. Was it always that loud?
16. I wish I could reach the TV dial without throwing Shannon onto the floor.
17. Is my leg asleep?
18. It's at least starting to fall asleep.
19. I wonder how far forward I could lean before I throw Shannon onto the floor.
20. I'm not going to wake this child up.

21. What time did Tom say he was getting home?
22. Maybe I could hold her head in place and slide a pillow to replace me underneath her.
23. I bet that could work.
24. I should probably just try to nap, too.
25. I'm tired but I have done nothing all dang day.
26. I bet I could reach that pillow with my foot.
27. Okay, I can grab that pillow's fringe with my foot.
28. Ow, ow, Charlie horse.
29. Don't scream.
30. Don't wake the child.
31. Is Charlie capitalized when you write Charlie horse and where does that name even come from?
32. Oh, fuck, point the toe up.
33. I should have eaten that banana.

34. Point the toe down.
35. It just smelled so gross, though.
36. Great, now I have to pee.
37. Maybe having two kids is a mistake.
38. They'll outnumber me all the time.
39. Maybe Tom will have a horrible workplace accident that will make us millions in settlement money.
40. I'd like to be settled.
41. But, you know, the accident wouldn't hurt him so much that he wouldn't be able help out around here.
42. Maybe it wasn't an accident? Maybe he has enemies?
43. Maybe we'll just win the lottery and get a butler.
44. Shannon moved her head and is it directly on my bladder now?

45. How does one even get a butler? Are those job openings listed in the classified?
46. I should open the window; the air is not moving in here.
47. Goddamn your pointy little elbows, Shannon!
48. That John McEnroe is such an asshole.
49. Gotta pee.
50. Martini and Rossi Asti Spumante, that's not helping.
51. I'm gonna have to move her.
52. Oh, shit, that's a contraction.

ELEVEN

"So, I'm probably not Angela. I was never really Angela. And I guess, I guess I'm just going to disappear then. I'm going to disappear into fucking nothingness before too long. Shit. Shit. I don't know-"

"Hold up. C'mon. You don't know that. Angela never thought she was, you know, mister Ilona. Maybe-"

"No. It's what makes sense. Angela got the memories and her brain processed them as dreams. I've got a bump on my head. Tyler slipped and fell and gave himself some brain trauma."

"And his brain rebooted from Angela's memories." Cliff rubbed his neck. "Goddamnit."

"Which means that, as soon as Tyler gets his head together, I'm gone. No home. Just gone."

"Now you don't know that! And you already disappeared and came back, so-"

"What am I supposed to do?" Angela looked at the car's ceiling. "What am I supposed to do?"

Cliff collected his thoughts. "Well darlin', I got three things to say to that. One, you went missing once for ten years and once for two years, and that's what already happened and you didn't even notice. At least it ain't gonna hurt. You know that much." Cliff sat, not sure whether or not to keep talking. But when in doubt, Cliff usually kept talking. "And thing number two, it's still just a guess. I mean, there could be a magic fish involved or a cursed ring or whatever. Until we find out different, let's just do what we want to do. Fuck it."

Angela covered her face with her left hand. She was rubbing her left eye with her thumb and

302

the right with her pointer
finger.

"Ah shit." Cliff couldn't
remember what his third point
was. He scratched his beard.
"Well, I'm here for you. That
wasn't gonna be the third
thing, but it is now." Cliff
awkwardly touched her shoulder.
"So, he said, "what would you
like to do today in the face of
oblivion?"

Angela laughed, which caused
tears to stream down from her
bloodshot eyes. "I just feel
beat up. You know?"

"Well, it's Sunday and I
'work from home' on Sunday,
which means I have roughly five
minutes' worth of stuff to do.
So, I'm free to take you
wherever you want to go. As the
fella says, the sky is-"

"The limit?"

"The only fence that we are
facing."

"I don't think that's how it goes."

"Angela, look at the goddamned moon and not the finger what's pointing at it. What do you want to do?"

She thought about this for a time. What did she want? "I don't know. I guess I'd like to listen to some sad music and eat a cheeseburger."

"Welp, it's 10 a.m. so the cheeseburger might have to wait. But I do got an app on my phone that has pretty much every song ever."

Cliff plugged a black wire into the bottom of his phone and turned the car keys toward acc.

"How about a little 'Live at the Old Quarter'?"

Angela shrugged. Cliff pushed and swiped at his phone.

The car speakers began to play, "A few announcements for

the people who just came in, other people have heard it five times-"

"Thanks."

"Not a problem. You want to go someplace?"

"Let's just sit here for a bit."

"All right." Cliff pulled the handle to his left and reclined his seat a bit.

After a moment, she asked, "How's my, how's Angela's, sister?"

"Shannon's good. She's living in Pasadena last I heard. Your dad's still kickin' too. He's always on Facebook posting those stupid memes with the minions on them. He, uh, hey are half these words making any sense to you?"

"Not really." She chuckled.

"Fuck it. Oh, shit." Cliff thought of something. "You know

what? You know whose wedding I went to last month?"

"I sure don't."

"Robert's."

"What? Did he marry a lady?"

"Naw, a dude. You can do that now. Nice Jewish guy from Texas." Cliff smiled as he said the word Texas. "Growing up gay and Jewish in Texas, you know that sumbuck must be tough, huh?"

"Actually, thousands of Jewish people from Eastern Europe settled in Texas due to the Galveston Plan. It was right before World War I, I think."

"See? You still sound like Angela to me."

Angela flopped her arm towards Cliff in a half-hearted attempt to punch him. "Shut up."

"Robert did tell me that he got the weirdest prank phone call with some crazy kid pretending to be you."

Angela laughed.

"Yeah." Cliff chortled. "I thought you'd know something about that." A beat. "You know he blamed me."

"I would've blamed you too." She smiled. "All right, sitting here is stupid. Let's go somewhere."

"Where to?"

"I don't care. I just need to move."

"I just thought of the place."

Cliff turned the key, momentarily interrupting the song "Don't You Take It Too Bad." He nudged the directional signal, and pulled back onto the road. They drove for a few minutes, until stopping at a convenience store.

He left the car running and said, "Wait here, as this is not the place I'm taking you."

Angela was about to tell Cliff to screw off when from the car stereo she heard, "this was recorded by Doc Watson, and it really blew my mind-"

"Fine. Can you get me a coffee?"

"-Loop and Lil were parakeets."

"Yeah, if they got it."

Cliff came back four minutes later carrying two coffees and a plastic bag. The bottom of the bag was contorted as though it were carrying an oblong box. He set the bag on the car's backseat and handed one of the coffees to Angela.

"I got it black, on account of you take it black. But I also got some fancy vanilla cream in case that's how Tyler drinks it."

"Fuck what Tyler wants," Angela said, taking a sip of the boiling hot coffee. She sniffed and wiped her eyes. She looked terrible.

"You okay?"

"Yeah. Old memories. Somebody else's old memories."

"Cool." Cliff backed out of the parking space and headed north.

Twenty-five minutes later, Angela saw it.

"Why did you take me here."

Cliff just smiled and said nothing.

"I said I wanted a burger," Angela said, staring at the rundown building adorned with the signage and logos of a Pizza Castle.

"Shit, you think we're here to eat? This place closed up three months ago."

"Well," Angela began but stopped when Cliff rested part of his body over her left side. She heard the crinkling of plastic as he pulled the plastic bag from the back seat.

"Happy birthday. Open it up."

She looked into the bag and saw two cartons of eggs.

"Yoko Ono once said that 'Violence is just one of those feelings that come when you are unable to communicate. Art is communication.'" Cliff grinned. "Old Cliff says, now is not time for art."

Angela smirked.

Cliff ran his fingers through his hair. "Well, come on, you damned delinquent. You know what to do."

Angela unbuckled her seatbelt, and awkwardly got up carrying the eggs. She set one of the cartons on the hood, and held the other one in her bent right arm. She grabbed an egg and tentatively threw it at the building that formerly housed the pizza chain. She threw a second egg with more confidence. The third egg shot out of her hand as though it were launched by a rocket. The fourth and fifth and sixth and seventh and eighth each smashed into the wall of the Pizza Castle, with less time between each splat.

By the time of the thirteenth egg, she was screaming with every throw.

Then she just kept on screaming.

Finally, Angela grew quiet. She rested her butt on the front of Cliff's car. She was sweaty and all out of eggs.

Cliff leaned on the side of the car, his arm resting on the roof. "I couldn't tell whether you'd be into that or not."

"Must the boy hormones. Makes you want to break stuff," she joked.

"Must be." Cliff said. His face grew mischievous with large, wild eyes and a half-smile. Angela thought he looked like John Astin about say something crazy and she thought about her dad. Cliff opened the driver side door and reached in, fiddling with something. "You know," Cliff began, "They are tearing down this place next week." The trunk of his car popped open. He walked in that direction.

"Now, I don't have my sledge, but I do keep a crowbar and a tire iron and bolt cutters in here. Oh and gloves, in case Tyler has them sensitive pinkies." He revealed those things by pushing aside a pile of canvas bags and undersized road cones.

"He does," Angela admitted.

"I thought he might."

312

Angela looked at the instruments of destruction with lust.

"Boy hormones?"

"Boy Hormones."

Forty-five minutes later, Angela emerged from the Pizza Castle dirty and dusty. Her hair was matted to her head, and her clothes were plastered to her body. Tyler may have had soft hands, but he had amazing cardio.

"Well I feel better," she said. "What now?"

"Now, we get ya a cheeseburger."

"Two cheeseburgers."

"Two cheeseburgers. After that, I was thinking you and I can do something together that I've wanted to do with you a long time." Cliff raised an eyebrow.

Angela flinched and said, "You're going to want me to shower first."

"We're gonna watch Star Wars, you damned sex pervert."

"Ugh, fine."

Angela left as soon as the droids landed on Tatooine. Tyler stayed to watch *Empire*.

MINUS TWELVE

"I think I might be pregnant. It feels like I'm pregnant," Linda announced to her half-asleep husband. She had started to brush her teeth and returned to the bedroom with her toothbrush still in her mouth.

"You'd know better than me," Tom replied, rubbing his eyes with his thumb and forefinger.

"I'm serious."

"Well," he sat up in bed. "Is it a good thing?" He patted a spot on the bed next to him to beckon his wife over.

"I don't know." Linda saw Tom's patting, and shot him a look that seemed to say, *I'm not a dog, asshole*. She continued brushing.

"Well, we've proven you can do it before," Tom said, smiling.

"What does that mean?"
Linda's words were garbled as
her mouth began to overflow
with toothpaste foam. She
looked around for a bit before
spitting into a potted plant.
She wiped her face with the
sleeve of her bathrobe.

"Well, you know." Tom
replied.

Linda sucked on the bristles
of the toothbrush before
putting it in the robe's
pocket.

"Well, I just mean," Tom
continued, "you can handle all
the baby stuff."

"You're smiling." Linda was
quite serious about this
accusation.

"Am I?" he asked, smiling.

"You're happy with this?"

"Well," Tom wondered how to
put it. A phrase rested on the
tip of his tongue. "I'm, uh,

316

what's that thing that Reagan says?"

"Cautiously optimistic?"

Tom pointed, as if to say *that's the one*. "I'm cautiously optimistic."

"I think you need more caution and less optimism," Linda advised.

"Yes ma'am." Tom stood up, wearing the bedsheet like a cape. He wrapped both his arms and the sheet around his wife. "You want me to schedule you an appointment with the doctor?"

Linda made a one syllable noise that told Tom, *it is early to see the doctor and I feel like I just had a baby and I hate going to the doctor and I don't want to do anything*. She squirmed out of his arms and the sheet.

"I still have his card in my wallet."

"You've got too much shit in your wallet," she said.

"That's true," he agreed.

"Can you just buy me one of those E.P.T.s from the drugstore? That way I can know in a few hours."

"Sure thing," Tom said, trying to hold back a smile.

"We can take it from there."

"I'll get dressed and go."

"Hey come here," Linda commanded.

Tom did that thing, and Linda gave him a quick kiss.

It was quite minty.

TWELVE

Angela woke up in a strange bed, but she was used to that by now. She groped the top of the nearest nightstand and found Tyler's phone. She checked the time and the year.

Saturday January fourteenth, 2017.

Angela got out of bed and looked into the mirror that was hooked onto the back of the bedroom door. "Tyler's looking pudgier," she said to no one in particular. She didn't recognize the room. It looked like one of those starter apartments, like the ones in the "student slums" when she went to college.

There was no bigfoot poster.

She called up Cliff. He picked up on the third ring.

"Jell-o."

"Hey Cliff. I'm back again, for who knows how long this time."

"Time-traveling Angela, I assume."

"Yeah."

"I figured as such. I don't think Tyler has ever used his phone as a phone before. Welp, how is you?"

"Well, you know," Angela responded.

"Yeah. Tell you what, Tyler is on my friend finding app. Hold up, I'm putting you on speaker. You there?"

"Yeah."

"It looks like I can get to you in about an hour, and I might bring a present. I mean, if you're up for it."

"Well, what else am I going to do?"

And so, Angela gathered whatever clean clothes she could find. She took a too cold shower where she had to bend down to get her head wet. She ate a package of brown sugar toaster pastries that were reasonably close to the name brand. Then she tried, unsuccessfully, to find the television.

She was looking through Tyler's bookshelves full of Japanese comics, when the door buzzer made her jump.

"Tyler," she had momentarily forgotten his last name, "Uh, Tyler's house."

At first there was no response, and then Angela realized that she had to hold down the switch marked LISTEN.

The voice cut in, "-sped a li'l bit, but nothing too scary, right?"

"Cliff?"

"Yeah. Buzz us in."

She did that thing, then walked to the apartment door. She peeked her head out and saw that she was on what looked to be the fifth floor. She watched for Cliff, then found him. He was carrying a large silver cylinder in his hand. Was that the present? He stopped and took a drink from it. Probably not. It was then that Angela noticed that Cliff was with a woman.

Was it Angela, the *real* Angela?

She heard Cliff complaining from a few flights away. "Tyler can't live in a goddamned elevator building, huh? Make my fat ass walk up all these stairs. Angela, darlin', get back in there, you're spoiling my surprise."

Angela did not comply. She thought it might have been Angela, but she didn't see any tattoos. Angela had tattoos. Those were real, right?

Cliff reached the bottom of the last flight. "Well, here is your damned surprise."

Angela finally got a good look at the surprise. The first thing she recognized were those freckles. Then she noticed the wavy hair, a little thinner and dyed a different color than before.

Perhaps most jarring of all was the face. It was just like her sister's but also like a real adult lady.

Cliff continued, "I done found you a Shannon. Shannon, you can pass me, I'm taking a breather. I'm sweating like a gigolo on Father's Day."

"Hey little sis. I'm going to give you a hug, but it's going to be sweaty."

She did that thing, and it was.

Angela led Shannon into the living room, where she sat on a large gray rubber ball. Angela backed into a slightly tattered couch that smelled like old Thai food. Cliff was the last one in, and plopped himself down on an office chair, saying, "It's enough to make a fella consider eating vegetables." He took a sip from his shiny travel mug and fiddled with the lid.

Shannon took in the room and said, "nice place you got here, but I guess that isn't really a compliment to you, huh?"

Cliff interjected. "Tyler remembers some stuff, so he might appreciate the compliment later. But I'll let you girls talk. I'll just be sitting over here, low key vaping."

Cliff pulled out a futuristic clear cigarette, and Angela concluded that he was low key vaping.

Shannon began, "So, how weird is this for you? I mean, it's weird for me."

"Hella-weird."

Cliff fiddled with his coffee mug and muttered, "How weird is it being anything at all." Angela shot him a look. Cliff held up his hand. "Ignore me."

She turned to Shannon. "Well, how have you been? How's dad? How am I? I kinda want to know everything. It's like learning the future, without any of the bad science fiction consequences of learning about the future. Does that sound crazy? I mean it is. It's all crazy."

"No, yeah. I know what you mean. I got a puppy once from a co-worker. It was one of those situations where they didn't know who the doggy father was. I mean, not to slut shame a dog or anything. But I would look at this puppy and wonder, what's he gonna look like? How big is he gonna get?" Shannon stopped and contemplated for a moment. "I guess, I do the same

325

thing with my son. Where are my priorities?" She laughed a long and loud laugh.

"You have a son?"

"He's going to be five years old in April." Shannon stammered for a moment, then took a breath. "I have a bunch of pictures on my phone." Shannon got up, took her phone out of her purse, and began swiping and scrolling. She sat down next to Angela on a thinly worn cushion of the couch and pointed the screen at her.

"There's Jack. We were just at the Rose parade. His dad's family goes every year."

"Where is he now?"

"With his dad."

"Oh, are you two still—"

"Oh yeah. No, we're all together, one big happy family, all that. I guess you know everything up until 2004?" The sentence became a question at the last word.

"More or less."

"Yeah?"

"Cliff tell you that I saw, um, me, um once? He brought Tyler-me to present day Angela me."

"He didn't."

"I ran away." Angela pointed at herself. "This me did."

"That doesn't sound like you," Shannon stated.

"Must be the Tyler in me."

"Do you think that the more often this happens that you get more like Tyler? Or do you think that maybe Tyler is becoming more like you?"

"Shit. I hadn't even thought of that. I guess it would be hard for me to tell."

Cliff chimed in, "I'll keep my peepers peeled in case Tyler

starts talking about Dave Foley or telling people that they meant to say lectern when they said podium."

"Thanks Cliff," Angela deadpanned. "I guess I still feel very much like 2004 Angela."

"2004. It's hard to keep track of the years when you're not in school. 2004, 2005, 2010, they all seem like basically the same year to me."

Angela remembered, "Well, in 2004, you were smoking a lot of pot-"

"Judge-y."

"And you kept on talking about moving to the Laos or something?"

"Thailand. You never did listen. I actually did."

"Listen?"

"No, the other one."

"You moved to the Thailand?"

"Yes. That was 2005. I can remember that much. I planned on staying forever. I lasted about three months in Chiang Mai. It is gorgeous there. Plus, my apartment was like $300 a month."

"That's crazy."

"I went a little crazy then."

There was a long pause. Angela counted the freckles on Shannon's nose. Were there new ones?

"How's dad?"

"He's snow-birding it. Has a crappy little place in Florida that he loves. He got remarried, and then divorced. You didn't miss much with that one. Huge bitch."

"Oh yeah?" Angela chuckled.

"Well, *other you* got along with her fine, but *other you*

329

doesn't have the same bitch sense as me. You know?"

"I guess you're right."

"Yes, I am right. Your big sister knows a thing or two, you know."

"I know."

Shannon sighed. "Sometimes I don't know."

Angela thought her sister looked like she was preparing to deliver a monologue. She knew the look well. Angela fed her sister the cue she knew she wanted.

"What do you mean?"

And Shannon was ready. "All your life, I've been trying to help you out, and all your life you've been rejecting me."

Wait. I'm not even the real Angela. I don't have to put up with this shit. I don't have to eat her shit like I've been doing for however many years.

330

"Look, I know we were never really like TV sisters who call each other every day and hang out all the time together and start a family band or anything. But I don't feel like I've been rejecting you. I've just been, you know-"

"You've been little miss self-reliant." Shannon looked proud and sad at the same time.

"What?"

"It's good for you. You're strong. It just, it just made me feel useless, you know? Like, I was trying to, well," Shannon stopped for a moment to choose her words. "I wasn't trying to be mom for you, but you know, if I could be, like, half a mom for you, maybe-"

"Maybe what?"

"Maybe things would hurt less." Shannon blinked deliberately, and dabbed her eyes with her sleeve. "I'm sorry. Enough of that."

"Don't be silly. It's okay. I'm not hurting." Angela looked at Shannon and realized it wasn't Angela's pain Shannon was talking about.

"If you couldn't tell by that little outburst, I've been to a therapist or four."

"Really?"

"Yeah. I was trying out a lot of things, I mean, a lot of things, but therapy seems to help the most. I mean, it's not perfect or even great, but," she trailed off with a high-pitched grunt.

Angela looked at her sister, and thought about the missing years, until she heard a loud slurping noise. Then, she remembered that Cliff was there. Apparently, he was out of coffee.

Angela turned her attention back to Shannon. She saw the lines around her damp eyes, her curly dyed hair and the even curlier grey hairs still peeking out.

"I guess I'm too scared to talk to real Angela like this. I guess, that's why I took Cliff up on the offer. You aren't the easiest person to talk to."

"I suppose so."

"But I shouldn't spend all this time here dealing with *my* issues, you know? I pay somebody for that. You want to know about what happens to you?"

"I don't know? I guess I do, some." Angela squirmed.

"Some? Well which some?"

"I don't know. Wait." Angela remembered something from her initial time as Tyler. "Cliff said something when I first called him. He said something like he used to know an Angela Brooks. At first, I thought I had died or something or disappeared from the past into the future. Or did Cliff just stop knowing me? Then I met me. So, Cliff didn't stop knowing me and I clearly didn't die or disappear. So, did I get married and change his name? That doesn't sound like me."

Cliff interrupted. "I can do this one!" He looked at Shannon and she nodded. "All right, you met this guy named Fred. Handsome, big head, tiny body, ya know, like a movie star?"

"His head was normal," Shannon declared.

"His head was the size of the prize-winning pumpkin at the Iowa state fair."

"Guys." Angela reminded the other two of her presence.

"So, you and Fred become a thing. And you move in together and realize that, what the hell, you want to up and get married. I think because the damned government and their societal engineering gives you a tax break."

"That was not the reason," Shannon exclaimed.

"That's the only reason to get married," Cliff declared. All right, Fred wants to have the same last name, on account of him hating kids with hyphens or some such. You say you don't want kids, but tell him that instead of taking his name why don't you both take a different name? Equality, feminism and death to the patriarchy. He says fine. He hated his fundamentalist family and thought that this would be a good way to piss them off. His last name was like Groupon or something stupid that he hated anyway."

"Grouper," Shannon corrected. "His last name was Grouper. And If I remember correctly, you wouldn't stop emailing Angela suggestions."

"Oh man, I almost got you guys to choose Bassett as your last name."

Angela smiled. "Fred Bassett, like that comic you hate."

"Oh my god, it's the worst comic!" Cliff exclaimed. "And Angela Bassett, which, frankly, is a lot to live up to."

"You are such an asshole," Shannon said, laughing.

Shannon interrupted. "Your name is now Angela Nelson."

"Goddamnit, Shannon, I was building to something."

"Fred wanted to do a wedding, and you ended up changing names before the ceremony."

"I also thought you should change your name to Robert's last name. He's got the best last name."

"Winberry?" Angela replied incredulously. "That's a terrible last name!"

"Then Fred ran out before the rehearsal," Shannon continued the story. "Didn't even take all his things from your house. He just flaked."

"Darlin', Winberry is the platonic ideal surname."

"I don't think that's right!" Angela disagreed.

"Anyways, I Facebook stalked him the other day. He's married and living in Vermont. You're prettier than her. Tyler's prettier than her."

"Tyler is a pretty man," Cliff noted.

"His wife just had a baby. I think that's what he really wanted. You never wanted that. I think you would've made each other miserable. On the record, though, I'm still angry with him."

"Thanks, I guess." Angela stood up and paced.

"Plus, the baby is ugly."

"Shannon, c'mon!"

"Sis, can I ask you, what's your plan?"

"I don't know," Angela admitted. "I feel limited in what I can do. I don't want to go out and get drunk and give Tyler a hangover. Though, I suppose there are worse things. I'm just a guest here, so I don't know what rights I have."

"Maybe, it's like being a kid," Shannon posited, "and you don't have any rights, but you don't have responsibilities."

"Angela, were you ever a kid?" Cliff asked.

"Shut up!" Angela replied.

"No, she wasn't. That's how you should think of this. Try to have some fun. Don't worry about tomorrow, because, well, you know."

"Who knows when tomorrow is going to be for you?" Cliff added, trying to drink coffee from his empty cup.

"So, be a kid. Well, I think I can at least manage that. Thanks, big sis."

"Mark it down, Cliff. Angela listened to me for the first time in god only knows how long." Shannon stood up.

"God only knows would mean that that's the only thing that god knows. So, really-"

Shannon hugged her sister. "You never change."

Now, Cliff stood up as well. He looked at the door. "I'm going to grab some coffee. There's a place right down the block. Give me ten minutes to get the coffee, and twenty minutes to make it back up those goddamned stairs. You guys want some? It's on me."

Cliff took the coffee orders and left; the sisters went back to the couch.

"It is good to see you," Angela said. The sisters sat for a moment in awkward silence.

"Really, though, what are your plans?" Shannon finally asked.

"My plans?"

"For this time around."

"I hadn't really thought of anything. I'm not sure really what I'm supposed to be doing. I don't think I'm really me, so I can't go back to my old body because it isn't really mine. And this body isn't really mine either. So, I guess I'm just supposed to chill."

"Netflix and chill?"

"I don't know what that means. Is that the mail-in video store?"

"Just listen to me on this. You don't need big plans. You need kid stuff. Go ride a rollercoaster, eat candy, play some video games, watch a movie. Or you could do other kid things and learn about this new world."

"This slightly brave, slightly new world," Angela said, dripping with sarcasm.

"Really?"

"No, you're right. Thanks," Angela forced a smile. "This, this actually, helps quite a lot."

It didn't.

Shannon smiled a satisfied smile.

And that actually helped Angela quite a lot.

"Oh, you know who I ran into the other day?" Shannon didn't wait for a guess. "Chris Kozminsky!"

"Oh, really?" Angela asked, pretending to be interested. "What's he up to?"

"I don't know. Working at EZ Pass or something, I think."

A noisy party.

"This is my friend Linda!"

"Linda, huh? You know Linda mean pretty in Spanish?"

"Yeah, but you say it leen-duh."

"Oh, and you don't?"

"Why don't you get me a drink, and start over."

"Sure thing, leen-duh!"

THIRTEEN

Angela woke up in an upright and seated position. There was a tiny window to the right of her, and out of that window she could look down and see clouds.

To the left of her, she saw a woman whose face she recognized. "Oh. Hey, Ms. Clark."

Tyler's mom replied, "Hello Angela." She was wearing a simple red shirt and what looked to Angela like black pajama pants.

"So, what's going on?"

Ms. Clark had a look on her face as though she were realizing something. "Tyler told me to tell you the date and year when-slash-if I saw you again."

"Okay." This seemed like a reasonable thing to do.

"It's March 17th 2018."

"St. Patrick's Day," Angela noted. "Are we flying some place festive?"

Ms. Clark looked sad.

"Oh, I'm sorry."

"My brother-in-law, your, Tyler's uncle died." She smiled one of those thoughtful grins that only happens when a person is sad.

"Oh, I'm so sorry."

"Well, he was suffering a long time and he's in a better place, now."

"I'm so sorry." Now, Angela wanted to apologize for apologizing too much.

"Tyler's dad is already there. He's helping grandma. I wish you'd be able to meet him under better circumstances. Well, if you are still with us when we see him. And well. . ."

"It's confusing. I'm sorry. I don't mean to be adding to

anybody's stress here." Another apology. Damnit.

"It's okay. I know, you're not in charge. And even if you are somebody else, you are still my kid and I still love you."

Ms. Clark's eyes turned redder at these words, and Angela felt like crying as well. She thought she was doing a good job of not crying; she wasn't.

"Now I'm sorry. I don't want to make you cry."

Angela laughed. She saw a tiny bag of Kleenex in the seat pocket in front of her and grabbed two. She blew her nose, and then offered a tissue to Ms. Clark. She took one and wiped her eyes.

"Oh, I was supposed to tell you to check your phone. Tyler's phone. Well, you know. Tyler said he never gets to talk to you, so he left you a message."

"Really?"

"Yes. He wrote you a letter in the phone. He said it was in the one folder. Um, Notes. Look in Notes."

Angela took the phone out from the seat pocket, and moved her thumb across the screen. It brought up news headlines. She tried again, and managed to open a camera application.

Ms. Clark saw her do this and became pleased with how she could be helpful. "Oh, you can just hold your left thumb on the button. It's fingerprints now. They're still all Tyler's fingerprints."

Angela did that thing, and searched the tiny, rounded squares until she found a program called notes. Near the top of a list of notes was an underlined sentence that said <u>For Angela</u>.

"Actually, you know, the new phones you are supposed to be able to open with your face. I don't think I like that." She looked down at the phone in Angela's hands. "Just touch there," Ms. Clark said. "I'm not supposed to read it." She opened her airline magazine and pulled a pen out from the seat pocket. She started filling in numbers in a nine by nine grid.

Angela read:

For Angela

Hi Angela. I don't think I need to say that this is a curious letter to write. I want to write to thank you for always worrying about what you're allowed to do in my body. I also wanted to thank you because it seems like you take over my life when I really need a break. It feels as

---

though you're a friendly panic attack. That's weird, right?

I wanted you to know that I'm still here. I know what goes on when you take over, and I don't mind to have somebody else do the driving. It's weird, right? When you get into a car, you kind of describe yourself and everybody else as the cars. That guy almost hit me! That guy is parked on top of me! Now I feel like my body is the car, and usually I drive it, but sometimes I'm the passenger. I passenge.

I wonder if we'll still feel that way when all the cars drive themselves.

But I digress, you haven't really overstayed your welcome… Yet! KNOCK WOOD.

I know you always feel like there's something you should be doing or shouldn't be doing, but don't worry so much about it. A friend of mine said that it's okay to not know what to do. We're all here against miraculous odds, and we all have a limited amount of time left. Science tells us that. You know? We are each a unique combination of one of hundreds of eggs and millions of sperm from two of the billions of people who each are also a combination of those things.

Sorry, it's hard to sound philosophical or poetic with all that sperm there. Sperm is limited to a very specific type of Irish poetry.

Physics is little less icky than biology (unless you ask Hannah). Did you ever hear that old song that says, we are all made of stars? That's, like, literally true. I just read a thing. The Big Bang started the universe, but only made the first three elements. Anything with a nucleus heavier than lithium was cooked up in a star. And I heard a scientist say that the atoms in your right arm probably came from a different star than the atoms in your left arm.

It made such an impact on me that I cannot remember his name. True story.

Back on topic: not only is it amazing that any of us are alive, it's amazing that you have this crazy time-traveling extra-life. Even if you are an echo of a memory, you're a double miracle. (Double miracle, what does it mean? (That is an incredibly funny reference, take my word for it.))

You're an explorer, a crazy future-naut.

I think by this time next year (As of writing, I have no idea when the reading will take place. Possibly never, in which case, I will have, perhaps, wasted some time.) I'll be older than you. That's going to be weird. So, take some advice from your soon-to-be elder: do what makes you happy, try not to hurt other people, help other people when you can, and you're made out of the dust of exploding suns. Don't feel bad if you want to spend a day on the couch watching Netflix. (It's through the internet now and much faster that way.)

And I wouldn't worry too much about being a memory. We all live in the now, which I've heard (from some other scientist whose name I can't remember) is somewhere between a few hundredths of a second and three seconds. Outside of that, all of us are memories.

Have fun.

Just don't give me a tattoo.

Your roommate,

Tyler.

P.S. You should watch Empire Strikes Back.

> P.P.S. If my mom asks, tell her this letter was about Jesus.

Angela turned off the phone and put it back in the seat pocket. She pushed the tiny button in the arm of her chair and reclined her seat.

"You doing okay?" Asked Ms. Clark.

"Yeah, I'm okay."

"Try to get some rest, okay, punkin?"

"I will."

Angela looked out the window of the plane. She could barely see the new moon in the sky and what looked like one of the Great Lakes below.

It was almost scary how beautiful everything looked.

"So, this homeless guy walks into a bar and he wants a free drink because he doesn't have any money. Because he's homeless. The bartender says, 'like screw you buddy; I don't give away free drinks. I work hard, nine, twelve, eleven hours a day.' Maybe nine hours a night. I don't know. He works hard.

"The homeless guy is like 'c'mon.' The bartender eventually gives up and tells the guy that he can have a free drink if he shows him something that he's never seen before. The bartender is like this super-jaded and has seen everything type of guy.

"The homeless guy is like, I got this, fam. He pulls a tiny piano out of his coat pocket and sets it on the bar. Then he pulls a hamster out of a different coat pocket and set

him on the tiny stool in front
of the tiny piano.

"The hamster starts playing
the tiny piano. Something
complicated too. Like the
Goldberg variations or jazz or
something.

"So, the bartender sets him
up with a drink. He's about to
give him a second one because
everybody in the bar is like
amazed by the hamster, when the
homeless guy is like, 'hey, if
I show you something else
amazing, can I get a second
drink?'

"The bartender is all like
'sure.' He was going to give
him one anyway, you know? So,
the homeless guy pulls a guinea
pig out of his pocket. He sets
it on the tiny piano. The
hamster starts playing jazz,
and the guinea pig starts
scatting. Like, the singing.
He's not pooping all over the
bar. You know like 'zee-ba-doo-
ba-do-wop soo pow!'

"One of the bar patrons calls up a talent agent. The agent says that he'll buy the act for a million dollars. The homeless guys is all like 'not for sale.'

"'Two million dollars.'

"'Not for sale.'

"Finally, the talent agent gives him a hundred thousand dollars just for the guinea pig and sets him up with free drinks from the bartender for the next month. They shake on it, the agent takes the guinea pig, and he leaves.

"The agent is cackling, like 'moohaahahaha.'

"The bartender is all like, 'buddy, why did you break up the act? You coulda won 'America's Got Talent' and you could have made millions of dollars?'

"The homeless guy says, 'the hamster is a ventriloquist.' And he gets a drink."

Silence.

"Huh?" was said in such a way as to imply, *what do you think?*

"I think I've heard that before with a frog and a rat." Angela stared at the road sign. The next rest area was 25 miles ahead. "You need to stop?" she asked.

"I wouldn't mind a coffee run. Well, I don't drink real coffee, but you know?"

"Okay. I could pee. Might as well get gas too."

"You want me to drive after that?"

"I'm okay for a little bit more."

"Just let me know," Tyler responded.

"Okay. Thanks."

Angela wondered if this trip was a bad idea.

They drove in silence for what felt like a long time. Needing to fill the silence, Tyler looked at Angela and said, "I'm writing a note to you."

"Okay. But you know that you can just tell me, right?"

"No. You know what I mean. I'm writing a note to past you."

"It's not really past me, Tyler. I thought you understood that."

"I do, but she is still your, I dunno-"

"Yes?"

"She's like a reflection of you or who you used to be. She seems real, and she feels real, even though she more like-"

"My echo?"

"Yeah! Yeah. Anyway, I know that it's not really you, but, you know, if you could give your younger self advice, well, what would it be."

Angela craved a cigarette. "I'll think about it."

"I asked Cliff," Tyler confessed. "You know what he said?"

"Stock picks, dinosaurs, and kill Hitler?"

"Yeah."

Angela scanned through the radio stations and found nothing she liked. She turned it off in anger. "How did Cliff talk you into this?"

"I wanted to go. It sounded like fun," answered Tyler.

"Really?" asked Angela.

"It is fun," answered Tyler.

"Really?"

"Angela, We're adventurers. We are on an actual treasure hunt."

That's what Cliff had called it when he had pitched the idea to Angela. It went a little something like this:

"All right, now this right here is a genuine opportunity at a road trip and treasure hunt rolled into one festive package. It's Indiana Jones meets *Midnight Run*. Hold up, I'll step back a minute. The date was September ninth, nineteen ninety. My aunt Judy marries her boyfriend of five years, Mr. Herbert Anderson. Now, this ain't the Stone Cold Steve Austin aunt. That's a different one.

"Mr. Herbert Anderson, he comes from money and he takes care of the two of them. Judy still works though, so she has a bunch of, what do they call it, expendable income? She gives the best Christmas presents, the good stuff with absolutely no educational value.

"So, Judy- disposable income. Not expendable, disposable. So, after a few years of this, she starts getting suspicious that this situation might not last forever. You know, like the standard lipstick on the collar and perfume smells or some shit like that. She needs a nest egg to ensure the lifestyle she has grown accustomed to.

"She invests and collects things and develops like a dragon's horde worth of treasure. Come the year 2000, she gets diagnosed with lung cancer, and dies right before 9-11 happened. I remember because that was the day her funeral was scheduled for, and 9-11 stole all her thunder just like when Lady Di croaked right after Mother Theresa. That bitch. Well, and then Herbert Anderson died a few years later, on account of he was a much older man already.

"Fast forward to this year. I get a dresser from my mom's

basement that used to belong to Aunt Judy. It's in lousy shape, so I take it apart to sand it and paint it, and I find a hidden compartment in the top drawer.

"It's got a key in it. This here key is on a ring that has the name and number to a storage facility. I call up the place, and it turns out that Aunt Judy was crazy enough to pay twenty years in advance. Now that payment was nineteen years and ten months ago.

"Unfortunately, I have several things scheduled that I cannot miss. So, I was thinking. . ."

"Did you ever notice that Cliff never actually goes on these adventures he sets up?" Angela asked.

"That's weird." Tyler answered.

"That's one word for it."

They got off the highway at the next rest stop, and both Angela and Tyler headed straight for the bathroom. Angela finished first and waited for Tyler next to a vending machine full of candy that looked like multicolored soccer balls.

Tyler walked right past Angela and directly to the claw machine. "Can you lend me a single?"

"You can *have* a single."

"Awesome."

Angela looked at the machine. Behind the glass there were ugly teddy bears, a keychain emblazoned with the N*Sync logo, stuffed super-heroes with stitches that looked crooked even from a distance, and motley collection of dollar store rejects.

"This machine is like the island of misfit toys for the

island of misfit toys," she said.

"Isn't it great?!" Tyler exclaimed.

"You going for the Odo?" Angela asked pointing to a plush Star Trek character.

"You refuse to watch *Star Wars*, but you know who Odo is?"

"Yeah. It's Rene Auberjonois. He was on 'Benson'!"

The machine gave Tyler three tries for Angela's dollar. He won the stuffed Odo on the second. He stuck his hand in through the hanging door and retrieved the plush doll. He handed it to Angela.

"You're giving me the Odo?"

"I only play for sport, Angela. It's catch and release."

"Gentleman's game."

The pair walked over to the coffee counter. Tyler ordered an iced chai, and Angela order a black half-caff.

"You like Chai, huh?"

"Well, it's sweet and I don't need all that caffeine of coffee."

"You know chai is loaded with caffeine, right?"

"Huh." Tyler sipped his drink through a straw. "I do now."

The pair walked out the automatic door. Angela held her coffee in her right hand and the tiny, plush DS9 shapeshifter in her left.

"You want me to drive?" Tyler asked.

"Nah. Why, you bored?"

"Just thought you might want a break is all."

"Thanks."

They got back in the car. Angela set Odo on the dash and her coffee in the cup holder. They gassed up, pulled out of the rest area, and got back on the highway.

This time it was Tyler who fiddled with the radio. He also found nothing he liked.

"Hey Angela."

"Yes?"

"Can I ask you something?"

Angela suppressed a number of sarcastic replies and simply answered, "Sure, ask me something."

"I want to know about the locket."

It was not a question.

The response, however, was. "Locket?"

"Yeah. My mom said that when I was you but not really you, I was asking about a locket. I

have hazy memories of being
you, but I can't remember your
memories that aren't also mine,
so-"

Angela felt like she had to
stop Tyler before he hurt
himself. "Oh yeah." Old
feelings returned to her. "I
wore that in college. It was
like my security blanket."

"It sounded really
important."

She sighed. "I guess I
entertained more romantic ideas
at the time."

"What happened?" Tyler
wondered.

"It's like Ally Sheedy says,
'When you grow up, your heart
dies.'"

"No, I mean, did you get rid
of it?"

"It's around, in a box,
somewhere."

Tyler turned his attention back to the radio. The stations scanned from a preacher shouting to classic rock and back again. "Was that from *Breakfast Club*?"

Angela smiled. "You got one, kid."

Tyler showed a look of pride, then turned off the radio. He took out his phone and scrolled through it with his left hand. He played with the switches on the right side of his seat, moving forward and backward, reclining and tilting. And so he sat, playing with his phone with his left hand and with his seat with his right.

The car was quiet for about five miles, minus the whirrs of the seat and the white noise of the air conditioning.

It was Angela who broke the silence this time. "It's okay to not know what you want."

"Huh?"

"This is my advice to myself. It's okay to not know what you want, and it's okay to not know what to do."

"Okay."

"I mean, if you have a goal, try to reach it. But if you don't, it's okay to just enjoy life. Enjoy your friends, your family, food, art, beauty, sex, and everything that we got in this world. It's all we got, and nothing is guaranteed."

"Should I be writing this down?" Tyler asked nervously.

"No, it's not that good."

"But this is like meaning of life stuff, right?"

"You know, I read once that only a fool thinks that there's only one meaning to life. It was in one of Roger Zelazny stories. A friend of mine got me into him. She got me hooked

on Zelazny and I got her hooked
on the show 'Lost'.

"I have since apologized."

They arrived at the storage
facility at five p.m. The place
was made up of rows of steel
garage doors, separated by
faded purple and tan walls.

"Which one is Aunt Judy's?"

"515."

The pair walked to the fifth
row of storage units.

Tyler looked at the numbers
as they walked and said, "501,
503, 505, I guess I don't need
to read them out loud."

"Sure don't."

They located 515. Angela
examined the lock; it didn't
look to be in any shape to
turn. She tried Cliff's found
key, tried it and was able to
confirm that suspicion.

"We might need to get bolt cutters," she said.

"Cliff said that I might want to bring some, but I don't know anybody who's got bolt cutters," Tyler admitted.

"Cliff told you to bring things?"

"He said he was Chucking this mission."

"Charlie-ing."

"Huh?"

"Never mind. What did you bring?"

"I'll go grab my bag!" Tyler responded with youthful exuberance.

He left, jogging toward the car. Angela leaned against the storage shed and checked her email on her phone. *How many emails does Best Buy need to send me?*

Tyler came back faster than Angela expected. He explained, "I don't have any car keys!"

He jogged a second lap, and returned with a royal blue backpack.

Angela examined it: road flares, flashlight, duct tape, three bottles of water, three granola bars, and something that Angela thought might help.

"You know, back in the day when I would go on one of Cliff's adventures, our friend Robert was the one who would bring all the stuff. He was a huge over-packer. I think he used to keep a case of bottled water in his car, just in case of emergencies."

"What happened to him?"

"He's in Cincinnati, last I checked." Angela removed the bottle of WD-40 from the bag, and inserted the red tube into the sprayer. She put the other end of the red tube into the lock and sprayed the lubricant inside.

She inserted the key, and it reluctantly turned.

"Help me with this door," she said.

Tyler did that thing. Then, he pulled the flashlight out of the bag, turned it on, and looked for a switch.

Angela pulled a string from a hanging lightbulb, but nothing happened. "Oh well." She motioned to Tyler in the dark. "Hey, shine that flashlight over here."

Tyler complied, revealing a stack of large blue Rubbermaid containers on the east wall, four across and four high. Each was big enough to fit a dead body, provided you folded it right.

"Dragon's horde of treasure!" Tyler exclaimed.

"So, which one you want to try first?"

"Top right." He was ready.

Angela took down the top right container and set it on an empty spot of the floor. She noted it wasn't very heavy for dragon treasure.

"Tyler, would you like to do the honors?"

"Yes. Yes, I would."

He handed Angela the flashlight. He grabbed the handle of the Rubbermaid lid and clicked it open. He peeled back the lid.

The treasure was held in about thirty clear plastic bags.

Angela had to laugh.

"Goddamnit, Cliff," Angela shouted, still chuckling.

"What kind of treasure is this?" he asked.

"The, uh, stuff that dreams
are made of," she answered.

"Huh?"

"They're Beanie Babies,
kid."

ACKNOWLEDGMENTS

Thanks go out to Karen and Matt Yaeger, for being the earliest readers of this surprisingly long process.

Thanks to Matt and Mattingly's Ice Cream Social and its scoops, for preaching fun and for not being a cult.

Special thanks to Joalton Newell for providing useful notes and being amused by my constant use of "that thing."